Star
Bright

A Novel by Sheila Tracy

Filidh Publishing

To my parents
Bernardine & Matthew Tucnik,

You dedicated your lives to family,
now I dedicate this book to you.

Sheila Tracy

Chapter 1

Sweat. She could feel one bead, in particular, poised between her should blades, slowly making its way down her spine, continuing down to the small of her back. That's where its journey ended, stopped short by the black crepe of the waistband of her dress. It was a very dramatic dress, with an elaborate, almost ridiculous hat to match. All of her mother's clothes had what you would call a certain flair to them. This ensemble made her feel like a little girl playing dress-up in her mother's clothing, especially as she was very tall and gangly and did not fill it out enough to do the outfit justice. The clothes were her mother's, but this was not a case of make-believe, in fact, the casket in front of her seemed all too real. The casket holding the very person who's clothes she was now wearing. Would her mother have approved? She probably would have said it was too sophisticated for a nineteen-year-old, but had she any choice? After all, her own wardrobe did not include anything suitable for a funeral. Her mother had always insisted that she wear pastels, or cute, theme inspired outfits. How she hated those clothes.

She knew what her mother had been trying to do, preserve the image of the little waif who had stolen the hearts of moviegoers everywhere. The little tomboy who, at the age of thirteen, had been nominated for an Oscar for her portrayal of a tough, yet sweet, street urchin in the movie "The Hobo's Daughter". Now that seemed like a lifetime ago, and a life that wasn't even hers.

Cassandra raised her startling green eyes from her mother's casket and, for the first time, took in her surroundings. Here she was, standing in a cemetery in East Los Angeles and she didn't like what she saw, or rather, what she didn't see. Where were all the trees? Sure, you could argue that the people laid to rest wouldn't know the difference, but what about the many mourners who passed through the gates? Not only could they not get away from their grief, but there was also no escape from the stifling heat, the heat that seemed to beat down with a vengeance onto the large, black hat adorning her head. Her head, oh how it was pounding, but maybe that was a good thing, the only evidence she had that she was still here on this earth. Ever since the news of her mother's accident and her subsequent death, nothing had seemed real. When she walked, it felt like she was floating through a dark tunnel, and when someone would speak to her, the voice sounded like it was coming from far, far away, like the voice of the minister as the service was coming to an end. "Ashes to ashes, dust to dust." With those words, the minister threw a handful of dirt onto the top of the casket. The sound of it hitting the hard surface startled Cassandra out of her trance and brought her sharply back to reality, but maybe too quickly. She felt herself falling deeper and deeper into a dark abyss.

Anthony's actions were swift and deliberate. He caught her just before her limp body hit the newly disturbed ground.   The hat wasn't so lucky.   As his arm slid beneath her shoulders, it caught the large brim of the hat, knocking it off of her head to expose the short, sleek copper mass of hair that had previously been hidden. It was at that moment that the press, previously held at bay, rushed through the line of security guards. The flashes of the camera bulbs were blinding and relentless, stopping only after the guards regained control of the situation, removing all members of the press from the grounds.

Anthony gave his head a shake, still trying to clear his vision from the blinding flash bulbs and lights from the press. He was a long time friend of both Cassandra and her mother and had been keeping a close eye on Cassandra throughout this trying day.   His guardian angel role started even before the church service. He had made a point of arranging it so that his car was the first after the limousine appointed to the family to follow in the funeral procession. That way, he would not be far away should his services be needed, as it turned out they had. Now that the rescue was over, and the gasps of surprise from the mourners had subsided, Anthony looked around for a bit of guidance. He hadn't a clue as to how to revive someone from a dead faint. He lifted Cassandra into his arms and headed in the direction of the cars. Once there, he managed to open the passenger door and place Cassandra in the seat. He then went around to the driver's side, got in, started the car and turned the air conditioning up full blast.

***

Why was someone trying to pull her out of her dream? She wanted to stay as she was, a little girl of seven. It had been her first audition ever. Her mother was off to one side of the stage, coaxing her on. She hadn't even felt nervous, just very excited. The excitement gave her an enchanting flush to her freckled face and an added brightness to her green eyes. How could everyone not help but be captivated? It had been her first television part, playing a female version of a Dennis the Menace type character. The sitcom was about a newly separated mother trying to cope with the extra challenge of dealing with a mischievous child who was always getting herself into some comedic form of trouble. Even more vivid in her memory of that audition was what followed that night. Cassandra, or Casey as she was fondly referred to back then, was too excited to sleep. Dressed in her polka dot baby doll pajamas, she tiptoed barefoot to her mother's room and slowly opened the door. She looked towards her mother's bed, only to find it empty. Then she caught a glimpse of her mother's long, auburn hair, lit up in the moonlight as she sat quietly by the open window. Her mother was dressed in a long, flowing nightgown of the finest cream coloured silk, and it shimmered when she turned and beckoned for Cassandra to come sit beside her.

As Cassandra sat within the comfort of her mother's arms, she looked up into the sky. It was that time of evening when twilight comes, and the first of the stars come out to do their twinkling dance. Her mother pointed to the sky at the first star to show itself that night. As Cassandra caught a glimpse of that star, she heard her mother say, "That is your star Casey, and that is where you belong, up in the sky with all of the other stars, to be adored by all. I want you always to remember that," and with those words, she spoke a slightly different version of a rhyme that Cassandra realized was redone especially for her, "star light, star bright, first star I see tonight, I wish I may, I wish I might become that star I see tonight." Almost upon the last words, Cassandra was fast asleep in her mother's arms.

***

Sleep, she just wanted to sleep in those arms, but wait, there were no comforting arms around her, just the sticky feel of leather on her back from the car seat. The air-conditioning had indeed done its job to revive her. She started to shiver. Anthony, who had long since discarded his suit jacket, retrieved it from the back seat and placed it around Cassandra. He started to drive away, only to be stopped by a rather plump woman, waving her arms wildly in the air. Whatever was that strange object she was holding? Anthony slid the window down as she approached. She was saying something to him, but Anthony wasn't taking it in, his focus was on, in his opinion, the ugliest looking hat he had ever set eyes on. The hat Cassandra had been wearing before she had fainted, now dust covered and trampled, was almost unrecognizable, almost. The woman was shoving it at him through the open window, and it seemed he had no option but to take the pathetic looking thing into his car. He quickly tossed it into the back seat and drove away.

***

The next morning Cassandra had thought that the worst part was over, but then she opened the front door. There, staring her in the face was, well, her face. She was front page news. Someone had taken it upon themselves to drop off a copy of "The Limelight", a Hollywood rag that everyone referred to as "The S'Lime". The nickname suited it well, or at the very least, the slimy reporters that worked for it. The writer responsible for this bit of trash had pulled no punches. The headline read, *Washed Up Child Star Fakes it in Lover's Arms*. She couldn't believe her eyes. The article went on to state that she faked that faint for the sake of getting sympathy from her former fans, and implied that Anthony was her lover. Cassandra couldn't help but think of Anthony and his wife and how mortified they must be. She read on. The article went on to make snide remarks about her apparel and appearance. Nothing like kicking a person when they're down! As upset as Cassandra was about the article, she had to put it aside and out of her mind. She had other, more pressing problems to deal with.

***

It was time for the reading of the will, and nothing could have prepared her for the shock that was to come.

Sitting across from her in the dark, oppressive office was Anthony. She was still so embarrassed by that disgusting article that she could barely look at him. Good old Anthony not only was he a longtime friend of the family, but he was also like a father to her. She never knew her real father. Her mother never spoke of him except to say that he had passed away shortly after Cassandra was born. There was always something in the tone of her mother's voice every time that the subject of her father came up that made Cassandra think twice about asking any probing questions.

Cassandra let her eyes drift to Anthony, and studying him now, tall, distinguished, always the gentleman, she couldn't help but wish he was her real father. Even so, she couldn't fault the way her mother had raised her. Sure, there were times when she was younger that she had felt like buckling under the pressure and wished that she could live the life of a regular kid, doing normal things such as going to a public school, making friends and just being a kid, but overall, she had no complaints. Her mother had always been very strong. Not only did she give constant encouragement to Cassandra, but she was also her manager, going out and getting the contracts for the choice parts that made Cassandra a child star. Her star had been rising and rising until the age of thirteen. But then, the inevitable happened, a growing spurt. She was no longer the cute little imp that had charmed millions. She had shot up almost overnight and had lost her childhood freckles. But the worst part was the rest of her development was slow in coming, making her no longer a child, but not yet able to play the role of a woman. Her mother had certainly had her work cut out for her since that time trying to secure parts for her. In fact, that's where he mother was the night of her car accident, talking to Carlyle Douglas, owner of the studio where she first got her start. There was a new movie in the works about a group of teenagers coming of age. The part would have been a perfect transition for her, or so her mother had believed. But now, her mother was dead, and so were Cassandra's hopes and dreams.

She turned towards the doorway as the lawyer, Jacob Sloan, entered the room. He was a short man with a slight build. He walked stiffly towards the head of the table, placed his briefcase down and opened it in one swift movement. It must have been fairly new, because as Casandra took a deep breath to steady her nerves, the smell of leather pervaded her nostrils. Jacob took his seat, and it was only then that he acknowledged Cassandra and Anthony. When he spoke, it was curtly and impersonally. There was no way to soften the blow Cassandras was about to be dealt.

The money was gone. Cassandra was stunned. How could that be? She had made millions in her short career. Jacob pushed his gold-rimmed glasses up on his pinched nose before answering. He explained that as good as her mother was at managing her career, money was another matter. Bad investment after bad investment, then the elaborate funeral arrangements had dwindled the money down to a mere ten thousand dollars. A thought hit Cassandra. What about the house? It wasn't quite a mansion, but it ran a close second and was on a prime piece of beachfront property. Jacob was by now feeling quite uncomfortable. He knew this was not going to be an easy meeting, but this was by far one of the worst situations he had ever dealt with. He cleared his throat and bluntly stated that her mother had never owned the property, the house, or even the furnishings in it. They all belonged to Carlyle Douglas, owner of the studio that had held her last contract. Even all the cars, including the one that her mother had been driving when she had her fatal accident all, belonged to Mr. Douglas. He owned it all, and now that there was no new contract in place, and there would not be another forthcoming, Mr. Douglas was requesting that she make other living arrangements. She would have three months to remove herself and her few belongings from the premises.

Anthony could not contain his anger any longer. The sound of his fist hitting the polished wood of the table startled both Jacob and Cassandra. "Bastard!" His outburst surprised even him, but he couldn't believe one man could be so cold and callous. When Jacob had called him up the day before and advised him to attend on behalf of Cassandra, he thought it was solely because Cassandra's mother had named him executor of the estate until such time that Casandra reached the age of twenty-one, but now he understood the real reason. He had been summoned to pick up the pieces of this shattered young woman.

As swiftly as Jacob had come, he was gone. Anthony and Cassandra sat across from each other in total silence, neither knowing how to break the silence, and neither did. With the lump that was in her throat, Cassandra found speech impossible, and Anthony thought that any words of comfort and encouragement would have seemed hollow and false. No, he would not insult her intelligence by uttering words of false hope. Even in her present state, she would have known them for what they were. Instead, he rose from the uncomfortable hardwood chair, walked around to the other side of the table and pulled out her chair, taking her hand in his, he helped her rise and find her feet. They walked out of the room, letting the heavy wooden door closed solidly behind them. The resounding noise it made lent a sense of finality to the whole sad affair.

"So how long has your affair been going on?" The comment was followed by the flash of the cameras' flash bulbs, out-doing the blinding sunlight. The press, like a pack of wolves, had hunted them down and were going in for the kill.

The silence in the car was a stark contrast to the chaos they had just fled. As the car turned onto the long, winding drive and approached the house, Cassandra looked, really looked, at it for the first time. The massive stone walls, the large leaded windows. Her eyes were drawn to one in particular. The one to her mother's bedroom, or rather, had been her mother's bedroom. Oh, what she would give right now to see her alive and vibrant standing at that window. But she knew it would never be ever again. As the car came to a stop at the large double front doors, she turned to Anthony to thank him, but the words stuck in her throat. He simply nodded his head in acknowledgment. Cassandra got out of the car and walked slowly up to the front doors. Watching her, Anthony's anger returned at the injustice of it all. He knew what he had to do to rectify it, and he drove away with a new-found determination.

***

Carlyle Douglas took in the richness of his surroundings. His office was deliberately decorated to impress those with power, and intimidate those without. One wall was devoted to a well-stocked bar, and another to tinted windows, the kind that you could see out but no one could see in. The remaining walls consisted of dark mahogany paneling covered with photographs of celebrities, past and present. Some were studio shots; others press shots, many of which included the celebrities at various events with Carlyle at their sides. He never actually cared for their company, but what he did like was how important it made him feel to be seen in their presence. Everything to him was about power. Even the chairs in his office provided him with it. Visitors would at first feel pampered when they were offered to take a seat in one of those deep leather chairs, only to find themselves sinking lower and lower as their host towered over them. If that didn't intimidate them, Carlyle's overbearing personality did.

Carlyle sat behind his massive mahogany desk. The chair he occupied was leather, but unlike the others, this one was not generously padded and was raised to a height that maintained his sense of power. He turned his attention to the papers in front of him. What agenda did he have today? Ah, he was about to fill out a pink slip for one of his soon to be former employees. Some things he just enjoyed attending to himself. He wasn't letting the person go until next week, but as usual, he was way ahead of himself. His wife always told him she was sure that if it had been possible, he would have sent out his own birth announcements when he was still in his mother's womb. Carlyle thought to himself how his wife thought she knew him so well, but there was so much his dutiful little wife didn't know about him, and he was determined to keep it that way. There, he was done. He put the completed form in his "out" basket, thought for a moment, then picked up the form and placed it on the edge of his desk. He decided that it would be much more satisfying to hand it to the employee in person. With a self-satisfied smile, he leaned back and waited for his ten o'clock appointment.

As he thought about the upcoming meeting, his smile disappeared. He had only met the man a couple of times while in the company of Carolyn Carrington. Normally he wouldn't have given the likes of Mr. Turner the time of day, but there had been something in the tone of the other man's voice that told him it would be in his best interest to hear the man out. Whatever it was, Carlyle knew he wasn't going to like it.

He looked at his Rolex and realized it was already twenty minutes past ten. He did not tolerate tardiness well. He buzzed his secretary and instructed her to look up the number of a Mr. Anthony Turner. If she couldn't reach him at home, she was to try to reach him at his office. He wasn't sure where he worked, but he did know that he was a real estate agent. She was to track him down no matter how long it took.

The order had come down, and Jane Templeton knew better than to protest. That's what he paid her the big bucks for, as he reminded her almost daily. Sometimes though she had to wonder if the job was worth it. She shrugged her shoulders, did a search on her computer for the name Anthony Turner and started her series of calls.

Carlyle was still fuming fifteen minutes later when his secretary delivered the news. She had reached the office where Mr. Turner works, or rather, worked. Apparently, the evening before he had suffered a fatal heart attack. After Carlyle had released the button on the intercom, his scowl disappeared as he threw back his head in a fit of laughter. He thought that things couldn't have worked out better than if he had planned it all himself. His day was shaping up nicely, and with a full half hour before his next appointment, he knew what he wanted to do. He reached for the pink slip he had placed on his desk earlier. This was turning out to be a very good day indeed.

***

Rain pelted her umbrella, bouncing off in all directions. As Cassandra stood looking over at the crowd of mourners, she couldn't help but compare today's funeral with that of her mother. Her mother's took place on such a dry, hot day, and here it was, just over a week later, wet and unseasonably cold. Today she was dressed as inconspicuously as possible and stood quite a distance from the ceremony. She was heartbroken that she couldn't be beside Anthony's family in their hour of need, but his wife had called her the night before, suggesting that it would be best that Cassandra keep her distance so that the press didn't make such an intimate service into a circus. She had to agree. She looked at the tear-stained faces and felt a sense of guilt. It wasn't that she hadn't been close to Anthony, after all, he had been like a father to her, it was just that having shed so many tears after her mother's death, she was literally out of tears. Her heart went out to his family, but she knew she could not comfort them. She simply had to walk away, a lone figure walking slowly into the distance, taking each step as if it were her last.

Her hands were so numb from the cold that she could barely put the key in the back door lock. With a bit of fumbling, she finally managed to unlock it, and then slipped quietly into the kitchen. Ever since she had found out that the house wasn't hers, she felt like an intruder. Besides, the house seemed that much larger and emptier when she went through the front doors and saw the grand sweeping staircase. She opted to go up the back stairs to her room and once there, closed the door. She looked at the door and wondered why she had bothered to close it as she already had total privacy. Not only was her mother no longer around but the maid had been given her walking order by Mr. Douglas.

She peeled off her wet clothes, wrapped herself in a thick terry bathrobe and proceeded to run herself a bath. She slowly lowered herself into the scented water. She inhaled deeply, taking in the fragrant scent of lavender. Lavender, she always found it so soothing. Maybe because it reminded her of happier times when she was a child. She had never cared for the expensive, heavy perfume that her mother always wore during the day, but when the day came to an end, her mother would have a bath scented with lavender. To Cassandra, it seemed as if her mother went through a metamorphosis with that nightly ritual. The hard-edged businesswoman turned into the warm, caring mother that she adored. She felt a stinging sensation behind her eyes. The tears wanted to fall, but they just weren't there. It was just as well because she simply didn't have the energy to shed any more. She climbed out of the massive tub and wrapped herself in a thick, luxurious towel that matched the green of her eyes. She walked across the marble floor and headed to her bedroom. No, it wasn't her bedroom, it belonged to Carlyle Douglas.

She was starting to detest his very name. To think that she actually had felt touched when she received his card of sympathy, expressing his sorrow in regards to her mother's passing. It has stuck in her mind because it was the first one that she had received. Then more cards had come in, most of business acquaintances, none from Cassandra's fans. It seems that they had long forgotten her. The cards she did receive she had no idea what to do with them. It wasn't like they were festive Christmas cards that you would put proudly on display, yet she couldn't just discard them. So instead, after she had read each one, she slipped them back into the envelopes that they had come in and placed them in a cardboard box. There they would stay until she decided exactly what to do with them. For now, that box was in the stack of other boxes that were packed with her and her mother's few belongings. The boxes were all ready to go but at this point in time, she still didn't know where those belongings, or she, would end up. She had never felt so alone.

Chapter 2

So, this was the beginning of the rest of her life. Cassandra let out a deep sigh. She looked around the tiny apartment and thought that, well, it wasn't much, but to her, it was now home. Located above a restaurant in East Los Angeles, it faced the street where she could see patrons of the restaurant coming and going. She took a deep breath. Mmm, the Chinese food that was cooking smelled so tempting, but she resisted. There was too much work to be done.

Night was upon Cassandra before she knew it. Where had the time gone? She had just finished the last of her unpacking and took a break by the open window. She turned her gaze from the activities of the night and took another look at her apartment and her sparse furnishings. One of her mother's interests had been collecting antiques, and those pieces were here with her now. She left the window and headed towards the bedroom. On her way she stopped briefly to pick up a pile of blankets and a pillow from a chair. Once at the bedroom doorway, she looked down at the bare hardwood floor. It was too bad that her mother's antique collection had not included a bed. She walked into the middle of the room and placed the pillow and blankets on the floor. Without bothering to undress, she laid down on top of them. Exhaustion had set in, and the discomfort of the make-shift bed went unnoticed by the sleeping Cassandra.

The sunlight wasn't direct, but it was still irritating to Cassandra's tired eyes. As she went to turn onto her other side to avoid the bright light, she let out an involuntary groan. Her body ached from the activity of the day before and from the unyielding hardness beneath her. What she wouldn't do for a bed right about now. Unfortunately, Anthony had only advanced her enough money to cover her rent and food for one month shortly before his fatal heart attack. Not being knowledgeable about legal matters, she didn't have any idea as to how to go about getting the rest of her money. She just assumed that it was going to take time and money, and she didn't have either. She was in dire straits and desperately needed to find a job. But where? It had been made quite clear by Carlyle Douglas that she wasn't welcome at his studio. She had made a few tentative calls to other studios, but it seemed that word had gotten around, and she had been blackballed throughout the entire acting community.

Well, just lazing about wasn't going to get her that job. She rose stiffly and slowly undressed, then headed to the bathroom for a very long, hot shower. The hot water stung but felt so good against her aching body. She dried herself off with one of the thick, luxurious towels that she had taken with her from the house. It was a gray area whether they had belonged to her mother or Carlyle Douglas, but she had defiantly taken them. After all, what was he going to do, come knocking on her door to get them?

***

Carlyle looked annoyed, but it was unavoidable. Jane Templeton braced herself to confront him and asked tentatively, "What do you want done with them?" Carlyle snapped at her "Done with what?" She replied "We have bags and bags full of cards and letters that have come in for Cassandra Carrington care of the studio. Did you want me to forward them on to her home address?" Carlyle's face began to turn an unflattering shade of red, and he retorted, "Trash them!" She blinked and shook her head in disbelief, "Pardon?" He shouted, "You heard me! Trash them! Get them out of this studio! I don't want them on the premises! Now go!" He then shoved her out the door and slammed it behind her.

She turned to the closed door behind her and let out a quite audible "Jerk!" Then she dutifully did what she was told and gathered up the bags of mail, but couldn't quite get out of her mind the image of a forlorn young woman who could be cheered by the tangible proof that people did care. Jane only hoped that Cassandra had a Facebook or Twitter account and could read how her fans sympathized with her loss, but Jane had her doubts. Carolyn Carrington had been very good at keeping Cassandra sheltered from the outside world.

***

Cassandra wasn't sure which hurt more, her feet or her pride. You would think that there would be some place that would hire a person that was ready and willing to put in an honest day's work. But what had she been thinking, going out to pound the pavement without a resume in hand? She had been naive to think that her name would have been enough to secure her a job. That was a laugh, some of the people she actually was able to meet with had never heard of her, and others just looked at her disbelievingly. But then, who would have room in their organization for a former child star? What kind of skills could she offer? She had never questioned her choice of career before, but now, somehow it seemed quite insignificant. It was time for her to get a "real job".

HELP WANTED. The sign was staring Cassandra in the face. Well, it was worth a try. She took a deep breath and walked in.

The aroma of Chinese food greeted her. To think she had spent the entire day looking for any place that might be hiring, and here it was, right under her nose, literally. It was the restaurant that she lived above. She crossed her fingers and hoped that the person doing the hiring spoke English because her knowledge of Chinese was nil.

Mr. Wing was a middle-aged Chinese man with a slight build who spoke somewhat broken English. He owned a family-run business, but his wife was in ill health and no longer well enough to wait on tables. He had trained all of his children, so he had no problem training one more person. Never having hired anyone before he had no clue as to what credentials to ask for, but she said she would work cheap and could start right away, so that was good enough for him. No, those weren't the only reasons. He thought himself a good judge of character and before him, he saw a young woman with a good heart. A sad heart, but a good heart.

She was hired. There were a few forms that Cassandra would need to fill out. She poised her pen above the first form. Surname, Carrington. First name, she wrote down Sandra. She wanted a new identity, one that would separate her old life from the one she was about to begin so she had started to go by the name Sandra. It was common enough, and it was actually a shortened form of Cassandra. It was the same name she had used when filling out the information on her apartment lease. She finished filling out the restaurant application forms and handed them over to Mr. Wing. She was to start first thing the next morning, at seven o'clock sharp.

Seven o'clock, well, at least, she didn't have to take travel time into account she thought as she climbed the stairs up to her apartment. So, a waitress. She couldn't help but think it rather ironic, after all, most actors started out waiting tables, not the other way around.

It was quite late, and she got ready for bed. Entering the bedroom she looked down at her make-shift bed on the floor. She crawled under the top blanket and laid down on her right side, then quickly onto her back and then onto her left side, then all the way back again trying to get comfortable. It was going to be a long night.

***

Sandra awoke with a start. What the?... oh, it was her alarm clock. It was six o'clock, time for her to get ready for work. Well, she didn't have to figure out what to wear. The day before Mr. Wing had provided her with a freshly dry-cleaned uniform. It was in keeping with the theme of the Chinese restaurant. It was made of a thick turquoise satin and was covered with embroidered dragons of gold coloured thread. It had a Mandarin collar and cap sleeves. Sandra quickly changed into the uniform then checked herself out in the mirror on her vanity. She thought that she looked ridiculous in it, her short copper hair not exactly reflecting an Asian ethnicity. She didn't realize that nobody would be taking notice of her hair, or what she could see in the limited view of her mirror. All attention would be focused on the long expanse of leg that showed past the uniform that was obviously cut for a much shorter woman. She squared her shoulders and stepped out of her apartment and down into the chaos of the restaurant that did not let up for her entire eight-hour shift.

What a day! Sandra's head was still spinning! She thought that trying to learn her lines for a new acting part had been difficult, try to keep track in your head of every single item every person had ordered at every single table throughout the day. Now *that* takes talent! She was totally spent. Back upstairs in her apartment, she shed her uniform, almost having to peel it off of her sticky, sweaty body. She had a quick shower, made herself a simple supper and made an early night of it, getting ready to do it all again the next day.

During the next two weeks, the days blurred into one another. At the end of it, Sandra was finally going to have something to show for it, a paycheque! It was Friday afternoon and at the end of her shift, Mr. Wing called her into his office. As she entered, he pulled an envelope out of the top drawer of his desk and handed it to her. It had her name on it, and she could see through the thin paper that there was a cheque in it. She thanked him and headed out the door and bounded up the stairs to her apartment. It was her first paycheque, and she had great plans for it. She tore open the envelope and looked at the amount. One thing for sure, she was going to have to revamp her plans, and those new plans did not include a bed in her near future.

The weeks came and went, and life became routine and boring. But it didn't really bother Sandra. After all of the traumatic events that she had in her life recently, boring was good. So time passed quite uneventfully until, one day, *he* walked in.

***

Although the restaurant was in an obscure part of town, it did bring in the occasional celebrity and well-to-do person. It was the perfect place where they could hang out and not worry about the press hounding them. The restaurant also had a reputation for great food. On this particular day, Fraser had decided to lay low after his jaunt to Monaco. Upon his return, his father, who always seemed to disapprove of whatever he did, had been more critical than usual of his extravagant gallivanting. He sat with his friend at a booth in the far corner of the restaurant.

Sandra had noticed him as soon as he walked through the door. She couldn't help but notice the fine bone structure of his tanned face and how it set off a complimentary contrast to his silvery blonde hair and pale gray eyes. He was sitting in her section, and Sandra made an unconscious effort to smooth back her hair before walking over to serve them. The attraction was mutual. Fraser was used to being surrounded by beautiful women, all polished and sophisticated, but the unadorned beauty in front of him, with her flawless complexion and sleek, shiny hair, did more to turn him on than any of those fabricated beauties. Sandra felt his eyes upon her and averted her eyes downwards, pretending to be concentrating on taking his order.

It seemed to be the day for the rich and the famous. Sitting in another section of the restaurant were Veronica Sutton and Chelsea Landers, two actors that were about the same age as Sandra. If she had heard right, were both auditioning for parts for the movie that her mother had been trying to secure for Sandra before the car accident.

Veronica had been keeping her eye on Fraser. Not that she was particularly interested in him, but he had connections, powerful connections, and she was looking for the opportunity to start up a conversation with him. Now all she had to do was wait until his attention was no longer on that stupid waitress. She focused her attention on her adversary. She didn't think of her as much in the way of competition, not a stitch of makeup on and a somewhat boyish hairstyle. Although she did notice that the waitress did have legs that she quite envied. Her scrutiny continued until her critical eyes came to the woman's face. That waitress seemed somewhat familiar. But where would she know a lowly waitress from? Then it hit her. But could it be? Was it actually Cassandra Carrington, the actress that about seven years ago had snatched the movie role from her? That was back in 2000; she remembered the year specifically because Cassandra had been nominated for an Oscar in 2001 for the role she had played in it. It was! She was positive that it was her. Veronica quickly whispered to Chelsea. Chelsea looked towards Cassandra, and both Veronica and Chelsea squealed with laughter and delight. Veronica got on her cell phone and made some calls. Then, she suggested to Chelsea that they stay and order dessert.

Sandra had just grabbed the teapot and was refilling Fraser's cup when they came barging in. She looked up and there it was again, the reoccurring nightmare. The camera bulbs flashed in her face as the press had a heyday. Mr. Wing came out of the kitchen when he heard all of the commotions. He was having none of this and quickly descended on the media group, a meat cleaver in hand. That and his threat to call the police had the press quickly exiting. There was no need for them to stay any longer anyhow, they had gotten what they came for, photos of Cassandra Carrington, former child star, reduced to having to take a job waiting tables. Their readers would eat it up.

After they had gone, Sandra couldn't contain herself any longer, she ran from the restaurant, hot tears of shame and humiliation running down her face. Veronica and Chelsea watched her go, exchanging smug looks; then they made their exit. Veronica didn't have the chance to approach Fraser, but overall she felt that she had accomplished enough for the day.

Mr. Wing hadn't raised four daughters without having learned patience. He took over Sandra's section himself. He thought he knew her character well enough to know she would be returning, and fairly soon. His instincts did not let him down. Ten minutes later Sandra walked back into the restaurant and extended her hand to take the order pad from him. As a father, Mr. Wing had also learned not to ask too many questions, and for that, Sandra was grateful.

***

Fraser had dressed for dinner, as was required when he stayed at his parents' home. He made a dashing figure, slim and elegant in his custom-made suit. He was expecting dinner to go, as usual, a bit of light banter from his mother until his father monopolized the conversation with his usual criticism of his son. Fraser shrugged his shoulders, years of this pattern had thickened his skin, and he was ready for whatever the old man had to throw at him.

The dining room was a picture of elegance. The white pristine table cloth was the perfect backdrop for the fine bone china and gleaming silverware, polished just that morning and every morning by one of the many servants. But this evening something was not quite right. His mother, usually ready with a cool put polite welcome, was unusually silent. His father, usually cold and indifferent was in a red-faced rage. Fraser wasn't sure what to make of this and decided just to carry on, as usual, taking his seat to the right of his father who was seated at the head of the table. His mother was seated to the left of his father, and Fraser acknowledged her with a slight nod of his head as he sat across from her. He had barely sat down when Carlyle Douglas took the copy of "The Limelight" he had been twisting in his hands and slammed it down on the table in front of Fraser. Fraser jumped back with surprise and shock, and not just from the force by which Carlyle had slammed the celebrity news magazine in front of him.

Carlyle barked, "What the hell is the meaning of this?" Fraser looked at his father. He looked even angrier than before, his face having gone from bright red to what could only be described as purple. Fraser looked down at "The Limelight" in front of him. The front page had a photograph of the waitress from the restaurant on it. Fraser didn't understand the connection. Carlyle raged on, "What are you doing with that woman? How long have you been seeing her and how serious it?" Fraser was dumbfounded. How would he make a connection between him and the waitress? He looked again at the photograph. Ah! There it was. The article made no mention of him, but there he was, in the bottom corner of the photograph looking up at the waitress, lust in his eyes. Fraser tried to explain to his father that he had never set eyes on her before that day, but his father wasn't listening. Carlyle continued on his rant, "Do you know who that is? That's Cassandra Carrington, all she would want from you would be what she thinks you can give her, a part in one of my movies! You are not to see her again do you hear me! Never! I'll disinherit you! Cut you out of my will, you'll get nothing!"

Fraser snapped to attention. He and his father had had many disagreements and arguments throughout the years, but this was the first time that his father had made such threats against him. He looked to his mother. She was looking back at him and on her face was a look of sympathy, yet as she turned and looked at her husband, Fraser could have sworn that she was actually enjoying the state his father was in. Fraser quickly tried to assure his father that he had no grounds for concern, that he wouldn't even go to that restaurant anymore. Carlyle seemed to have calmed down significantly, and his face remained only slightly flushed. The first course of the meal that the servant had been holding off until things calmed down was now brought in. The entire meal was eaten in silence with everyone left to their own thoughts.

Fraser's thoughts were of Cassandra. So, Cassandra Carrington, that's who she was. Fraser had noticed that her name tag said Sandra, so it did fit. Fraser had finally stopped reeling from his father's wrath, and now he was intrigued. He had never seen his father so impassioned by anything before. This just made Fraser want to defy him all the more. Of course, he would have to do it behind his back. This called for some cunning. He couldn't ever have the two meet, so he would have to make up a false background, go by another name. It would be easy enough to set up an apartment. He certainly had the funds at his disposal and money talks. There had to be at least one vacancy he could take advantage of, no questions asked. He would just need to find a place that had all utilities included, so he didn't need to have any bills in his name for water, heat and electricity. A phone would be no problem; a burner phone would be easy enough to get. He had it all figured out in his mind. He was on his way to seducing the young, sweet Miss Carrington.

Charlotte Douglas glanced at her son across the dinner table. Her son who took after her in so many ways, the same silvery blonde hair, pale gray eyes, and bone structure. They were two of a kind, and she knew him as well as she knew herself. She thought of how many times throughout the years she had seen that look on his face. Actually, it was a series of looks. First the defiance, then the serious concentration which always led to a self-satisfied smile once he had worked things out to his advantage in his mind. He was going to pursue the young Carrington woman. She stole a glance towards her husband. He was so arrogant he would never believe in a million years that his son would defy him, especially with the threat of being disinherited. This could prove to be the one situation that was going to be the undoing of Carlyle Douglas, and Charlotte was going to make sure that she didn't miss any part of it, and would enjoy every minute of it. She went back to her meal, eating in silence.

***

Fraser was putting his plan into motion. He had looked at several apartments and thought that he had finally found the perfect one. It was located just off of Wilshire Boulevard, not too upscale and certainly not of the grandeur he was used to, but it was pleasant enough. But of utmost importance, the landlord did not ask any questions. That's the way it goes when you hand over a wad of cold hard cash. Furnishing it was no problem either as there were a number of shops and department stores close by. Again, he went for items that were not too upscale and paid cash. Fraser looked around the moderately sized flat. It was perfect, perfect in that it was nondescript. Now, all he needed was a nondescript identity to match. Fraser Douglas. Now how could he change that? His first name would be easy enough to change. Most of his friends call him Zack, short for Zachary, his middle name. But what if he were to run into someone who called him Mr. Douglas? He would have to choose a name that sounded similar, that way it would just seem that someone had just mispronounced it, or not quite gotten it right. He racked his brain, but the best he could come up with was Dungess. Yes, Zack Dungess would have to do. What kind of job could he fabricate? It couldn't be in an actual office, after all, women always want to at some point in time drop into their man's workplace. Ah, a free-lance writer, something he could supposedly do from the comfort of his home. Everything was in place, now all that was left for him to do was to introduce himself to Cassandra Carrington.

He thought back to the first time he had ever seen her. She must have been about seven years old when she had auditioned for his father. She had been so out-going, and Fraser had been envious of her. Not only for the fact that he wished it was him out on that stage, but that she had his father's full attention, something that he had never had. She didn't see him there that day; nobody had, not even his father, *especially* not his father. Carlyle Douglas had made it quite clear that he did not want his son "in the business". His father never did believe that he had any talent as an actor, so instead he did nothing. Oh, he traveled abroad a lot, it was his father's way of keeping him out of his life, not to mention out of the spotlight. Fraser said to himself, "Well dad, it's too bad you're not going to see just how good an actor your son can be because I plan on playing this role to the hilt!"

***

It had finally arrived. After being deprived of one for so long, Sandra felt almost guilty splurging on it. But then she thought of her aching bones and decided that yes, she was entitled to a big luxurious bed. And she had definitely worked hard for it, two month's wages to be exact. She didn't know why she had gone all out on one, after all, a king-sized bed just for her? Maybe subconsciously she was hoping that she wouldn't be alone in it for long. Even after that terrible day when the press had shown up at work, all she could think of at the end of that day was the slim, elegant man with the pale hair and light gray eyes. She slipped between the sheets, and as she drifted off to sleep, her dreams took over, dreams dominated by a knight in shiny armour. The brilliant metal of the armour gleamed in the moonlight, but it was outshone by her hero's silvery blonde hair.

Chapter 3

It was a day from hell. Sandra hadn't slept well the night before, and the fluorescent lighting in the restaurant hurt her eyes. She could swear that every pervert in the vicinity picked today to patronize the place. And wouldn't you know it, her boss had decided to take the day off. At least, when he was around, he kept any undesirables at bay. Sandra had to lean far into one of the booths to serve a customer their order, and as she did so, one of the more obnoxious patrons came up to her and groped her from behind. It startled her so much that she swung around with the plate of food still in her hand. The food went flying into the face of the customer she had been about to serve. The plate crashed to the floor, stopping all conversation. All eyes were on Sandra as she apologized to the customer profusely, but to no avail. The man rose from the table and left in disgust. The man who had been the cause of it all sneered, called her a "useless bitch", and left the restaurant without paying. Sandra didn't even care at that point; she was too busy on her hands and knees cleaning up the mess of food and the broken plate. She managed to get it all onto a tray and got up from the floor. As she headed towards the kitchen, two patrons walked by, Veronica Sutton and Chelsea Landers. They didn't acknowledge Sandra, but as they passed, Veronica said to Chelsea, "Good help is so hard to find these days." and they left the restaurant with self-satisfied smiles.

Sandra, with her head down, entered the kitchen. She dumped the contents of her tray into the garbage and sat down on a stool. The doors to the kitchen kept swinging open as Mr. Wing's daughters went to and fro, going about their business, and Sandra could hear the loud din of the crowd mixed with the clattering of cutlery and china. She knew she should get back out there, but she just did not want to move. Ling, the youngest daughter, approached her and told her that there was someone out front at the cash register asking for her. She gave Sandra an encouraging smile, then continued on with her duties. With dread, Sandra got up, walked through one of the swinging doors and headed to the cash register.

The man did not look familiar. Had she served him earlier? As she got closer, she noticed a large package under his arm. "Are you Sandra?" he inquired. Sandra nodded her head. As he handed over the large rectangular box, he said: "These are for you." Puzzled, Sandra opened the box. She held her free hand up to her face, overwhelmed by the sight. Inside the box were a dozen beautiful long-stemmed white roses. Some of them were in full bloom, showing their soft velvety petals, others were budding beauties, their full potential yet to be revealed. They were lying on a bed of greenery. Sandra, not wanting to disturb the bouquet's loveliness, picked up just one single dewy rose. She cradled it in her hand and breathed in its heady scent. Then she came back to reality.

Sandra thought that it must be a mistake. Who would be sending her flowers? By this time, all of Mr. Wing's daughters were milling around her, all curious as to who her admirer was. Then she noticed it, the small card, tucked into the bottom corner of the box. Written with a flourish was, *Please honour me with your presence at dinner tonight. Meet me at the restaurant at seven o'clock* and it was signed *Zack*. Sandra was intrigued and excited. As a child star, she had received many flowers on various occasions, but never in a romantic context. She had butterflies in her stomach as she anticipated the night ahead.

Sandra's shift didn't end for another hour, but all four daughters encouraged her to take off early to give her time to get ready for her big date. Sandra didn't even think twice. She left the restaurant and headed upstairs to her apartment, feeling like she was floating on air.

***

Karen was just leaving her apartment to go to work. She was locking her door when she spotted Sandra coming up the hallway to her apartment, a bouquet of white roses in her arms. Karen had only talked briefly with Sandra a few times. They actually got on quite well, but with her odd shifts at the hospital, they simply didn't have the chance to chat as often as they would like. Karen yelled down the hallway, "Big date tonight?" and then headed towards Sandra. Sandra nodded and blushed. "Well don't do anything I wouldn't do." and with a wink and an encouraging smile to Sandra, Karen headed off to work.

Karen was relieved to see Sandra so happy. She really didn't know much about Sandra as she didn't offer much information about herself, but from what Karen did know, she had put Sandra on her "good heart" list. She also had a sneaking suspicion that Sandra had gone through a lot lately and figured that was the reason Sandra was silent on some aspects of her life.

***

No, that wouldn't do. Certainly not that, or that either. Sandra was at her wits end deciding what to wear. She hadn't even bothered looking through her own outfits but had gone straight to her mother's clothes. Everything was just "not her". She discarded each item one by one until she came upon a midnight blue silk dress. It was a slim, sleeveless dress with a draped neckline. She slipped the dress on over her head, and the slinky material slid down her body. She stole a glance in the mirror and studied herself. Her neckline looked so bare. Her mother's pearls, they would be perfect! She opened a dresser drawer and sifted through the various scarfs and gloves. Ah, there they were. She opened the black velvet case and lifted the creamy orbs to her throat. Her hands were trembling as she fastened the silver clasp. Not one for makeup, she had kept it simple with just a bit of blush, mascara, and clear lip gloss. She grasped the elastic band that had held her hair all day and pulled, releasing her hair from its confines. It had grown quite long in a short period of time, and now it swung down, its silky softness caressing her bare shoulders.

Sandra looked at the time, 6:50 pm. She grabbed her clutch and was heading out the door when she stopped short. Shoes! She rushed back into the bedroom and got down on her hands and knees. Black? No. White? No. She had gone through green, red, gold and brown before she decided on the high-heeled sandals in a dull pewter colour. She fastened the straps and was on her way.

Sandra picked her way carefully down the back stairway and rounded the corner to the front of the restaurant. She smoothed her hair and her dress, then tentatively walked through the door. She looked around but didn't even know who she was looking for. She was intrigued, who was this Zack? Would she be attracted to him? She went to take a couple of steps further into the restaurant when she caught a white blur out of the corner of her eye. It was a perfect white rose, and holding the rose was a man with silvery blonde hair. It was him, the man of her dreams, her knight in shining armour, and he had arrived just in time to sweep her off of her feet. He smiled, showing a blaze of white teeth that contrasted sharply with his tanned face, and said, "Good evening, I'm Zack, Zack Dungess." She returned in kind, "Sandra Carrington." He took her hand and held it to his lips, and Sandra blushed with both embarrassment and pleasure. Zack said, "I hope you don't mind, but I made dinner reservations elsewhere. After working here all day I thought you would like a change of scenery." She nodded her agreement, and they went out the doors into the cool night air.

He led her to a waiting taxi. He opened the door, helped her into the taxi and then slid in beside her. He gave the driver an address on Melrose Avenue and once there was a break in the traffic they were on their way. Zack had decided it would be best if he didn't use his own car. His Lamborghini would have been too high-end for the role of the man he was playing, so he gave the excuse that he preferred to use taxis rather than own a vehicle. Zack didn't give a second thought as to how pricey this would become, money was no object.

The taxi pulled up in front of a seafood restaurant. Zack had heard of the restaurant's reputation as a cozy, romantic rendezvous spot and that was exactly what he was looking for. He needed to be discrete.

Sandra found the restaurant to be a pleasant surprise. Dark blue linen table cloths covered the small tables that were only large enough to seat two. The flickering light from the white tapered candles cast a warm glow throughout the restaurant. They didn't have to wait for their table and were ushered right in. Once seated they were handed menus and a wine list. Sandra was baffled by the wine list. She had only been allowed a bit of wine on special occasions such as at Christmas but never paid any attention to what kind she was drinking.

She focused her attention on the food menu. It wasn't the most expensive place, but she still thought the entrees to be pricey. She decided to go with the lobster pot pie. Zack ordered the surf and turf and a bottle of wine for the two of them to share. They had chatted in the car on the way to the restaurant, but now, with the waiter gone and being face to face with Zack, she was suddenly tongue-tied. Zack could see Sandra's sudden nervousness and quickly tried to put her at ease, telling her a bit about himself, well, not about his real Fraser Douglas self, but about his newly invented self, Zachary Dungess. He told her about how he had been abroad for the last few years, working as a freelance writer in France and Italy. He chose those countries as he had actually been to both countries several times, and he had a captive audience as he talked about their climates, scenery, and the people. He went on to talk about his freelance work in those countries, how he would travel to small villages to conduct interviews with the local residents and write short human interest stories about them. The lies flowed out of Zack's mouth, surprising even himself as to how easily he was able to make those lies sound so convincing.

After their meal, they were both tempted by luscious desserts. Zack took advantage of the break to turn the conversation to her. He already knew everything about Cassandra Carrington, but he couldn't very well admit it without throwing suspicion his way, so he again played his part, asking questions and listening intently to what she had to say. Maybe it was the wine, but Sandra found herself opening up enough to tell him who she was, Cassandra Carrington. Zack reacted with a surprised, "Not *the* Cassandra Carrington! Why I saw your movie 'The Hobo's Daughter' three times! But why aren't you making more movies right now?" he asked innocently. Sandra thought before she answered the question. She really didn't want to go into all the nasty little details, so she simply said that since her mother had passed away, she hadn't felt up to it and that maybe sometime in the future she would consider getting back into acting. Zack simply nodded his head and accepted the answer as she gave it, after all, he pretty much already knew the real story.

It was ten o'clock by the time they were ready to leave and, as charming as Sandra looked, Zack could see that she was all done in. Not wanting to scare her off, he decided it best to play the perfect gentleman and dropped her off without even giving her a goodnight kiss.

***

Sandra's legs felt like jelly, and she had to lean against the door she had just closed behind her. Was it nervousness? Exhaustion? Excitement? Or simply the effect of the wine? Whatever it was, it had the strangest effect on her. She undressed and slipped into bed, a bed that suddenly felt way too empty.

***

It wasn't that Karen wasn't happy for Sandra, but she couldn't help but feel that things were moving too fast in this relationship between Sandra and this man she kept going on about. Karen was only six years older than Sandra, so it didn't take much to remember what it was like to be nineteen. An age where you found your freedom and were ready to get out there and experience life. You thought you knew it all and felt invincible. But was Sandra ready for it? She just seemed so naive. Karen shrugged her shoulders; maybe she was being over-protective and paranoid. It was probably due to the fact that she had never actually met this man, and therefore, not able to form an opinion of him. She looked out her window that faced the street but just managed to catch a glimpse of the taxi as it pulled out into traffic.

***

It was in the air. Sandra felt it throughout her entire body, an electrical charge that made every fiber of her being tingle. She looked into Zack's light gray eyes, and it was as if sparks flew from his eyes to hers. They both had no doubt in their minds that tonight was the night. Sandra was almost breathless as Zack reached out to touch her, and when he did, his hands had the effect of hot flames on her skin. The warmth spread throughout her body, melting away any remaining inhibitions, leaving behind only molten lava, mounting inside of her, edging closer to the surface, ready to explode. And it did! Her body was awash in a sea of passion; the ocean roared in her ears as the waves washed over her again and again.

Zack cradled her in his arms and kissed her soft, damp hair. He was at a loss for words. He thought back to all of the women he had been with in the past, and not one of them even came close to being capable of the raw, honest passion that Sandra possessed.

With their bodies entwined, they each fell into a deep sleep. But the sleep did not last, as their bodies, so attuned to each other, awakened to seek each other out again. The night did not belong to them, it was ruled by their insatiable passion, never stopping until the light of dawn. It was only then that their bodies would rest.

***

She felt like she was living in a dream. Sandra rolled onto her back and stretched luxuriously. Zack had just left to get them something for breakfast at a nearby cafe, so she took advantage of the privacy to make her way to the bathroom, not bothering to put on her clothes. She tentatively looked in the medicine cabinet mirror. Odd, she didn't look any different, but she sure felt it. She felt alive!

***

There was no way that he was going to give her up! Zack, with coffee and croissants in hand, headed back to his apartment. He was racking his brain as to how he could keep seeing Sandra without being found out. He had managed so far, but with Christmas fast approaching, it was going to be harder and harder for him to keep her away from his usual haunts, especially as the invitations for galas would be showing up soon. And then there were his parents, they would be expecting him for Christmas dinner. How could he not show up there, or if he did, how could he explain to Sandra that she wasn't invited? There was no way that he could let her know his real identity and no way that he could let his father know that he was seeing her. He would have to figure it all out later, right now he was approaching his apartment, and his thoughts were turning to other, more pleasurable things.

***

They couldn't get enough of each other. Every moment they could manage to spend together, they did. When Sandra wasn't at work, she spent most of her time at Zack's place. That's where she was now, waiting for him to return from a short errand he had to run. He was taking quite a while, and she was getting restless and bored. She got up from the sofa and went over to the bookshelf located against the far wall. There were encyclopedias, a dictionary, and a thesaurus. All the kinds of books you would expect a writer to have. She would have expected them to be more worn, but they all seemed so new. She thought that perhaps he found it faster and easier to do research on the Internet rather than physically flipping through pages. A stack of magazines caught her eye. She started to sift through them, hoping to find some that might contain some of Zack's work.

The door had opened, but Sandra didn't notice. She was so engrossed in studying the magazines spread out in front of her that she actually jumped when Zack put his hands over her eyes and whispered in her ear "Miss me?" She raised her hands up to his, which were still covering her eyes, but when she went to remove them, he just laughed and told her to trust him. Zack then led her to the sofa where he had her sit down. Once seated he uncovered her eyes and quickly reached into his pocket to pull out his surprise. Sandra opened her eyes and focused on what was in front of her, and then her eyes widened with excitement. Two tickets to New York City. It was fantastic! She had never been to New York, and now she was going to be there for Christmas and New Year's Eve! New Year's Eve in Times Square with the man she loved! Life couldn't get any better than this! She wrapped her arms around Zack, and he caught her to him, lifting her up off of the sofa and spinning her around the room until they were both light-headed and dizzy. They ended up on the floor and, still in their embrace, took their closeness to a higher level. They didn't have to wait until New Year's Eve to experience fireworks!

***

The snowflake drifted down, landing, then melting on her tongue. Sandra squealed with delight. She had never seen snow before. Well, of course, she had seen it on television, in photographs, and on Christmas greeting cards, but this was different! She, though, you don't just see snow, you feel it, you embrace it! She tilted her head as far back as she could and looked up into the sky. The snowflakes came straight at her, like thousands of shooting stars heading towards her, but in slow motion. It was mesmerizing!

Zack couldn't help but smile. He could have watched her all day, looking at her flushed face, her glossy hair, held back from her face with a knit headband that was now barely visible as the snow accumulated on it. He took in her slim figure as she swooped down to gather a handful of snow from the ground. Then it hit him, splat! Right in the center of his forehead. He looked at her in disbelief. A snowball! She had thrown a snowball at him! He retaliated quickly, and neither of them showed any mercy as they pelted each other with wet slushy blobs, every man, and woman for themselves! It ended in a truce with them walking hand in hand back to their hotel room, both eager for a greater surrender.

***

It was Christmas Eve and the streets, and the stores were packed with last minute shoppers, Sandra included. How could she have let the time slip away? Now she was in a panic as to what to get Zack for Christmas. Her funds were limited and limited her choices. There was still a great selection in the stores, but everything was so expensive. Just when she thought she couldn't stand one more minute of being jostled around by the crowds, she saw it. She looked up at the name on the store, then winced. This gift was going to be a big hit to her bank account.

Sandra walked out of the store, purchase in hand, and had actually managed to come away with some of her money still intact. Now with the pressure off, she was able to stroll along at her leisure and enjoy the sights. It had been snowing for quite a while, and the snow had accumulated on everything it had landed on, including all of the trees. No matter where she turned, Christmas lights twinkled back at her, and baubles glittered almost as bright. It was a winter wonderland! All of a sudden she felt like sharing it. She hid the gift in her shopping bag that held a few small purchases she had made earlier, then went off to find Zack.

***

This Christmas was certainly different than any Sandra had ever experienced before. No traditional Christmas tree, no turkey being prepared in the kitchen, and, of course, the largest void was the one left by her mother's absence. But at the same time, she felt fortunate to have someone special to share it with. She turned her body towards the man in bed beside her. A strand of silvery blonde hair covered one eye, and Sandra brushed it back, replacing it with feather-light kisses. She moved her body over to his as her kisses traveled down his body, down until her lips reached their final destination. Zack awoke with a moan.

✳✳✳

Some time later Zack whispered in Sandra's ear, "Merry Christmas baby." He reached into the top drawer of his bedside table, grabbed a wrapped gift and handed it to her. Sandra untied the silver coloured ribbon and lifted the pale blue lid. She gasped at the dazzling brilliance of the line of diamonds that made up the tennis bracelet. It was divine. Zack lifted it out of the box and fastened it around her slender wrist. Sandra, as thanks, gave him a slow sensuous kiss. She then reached beneath the bed and started to feel around, ah, there it was! She grabbed the present and handed it to Zack and said, "I'm afraid my gift is going to seem insignificant compared to yours." He lifted the lid and admired the tasteful ID bracelet, engraved with his name, *Zachary*. The sight of the name in front of him hit home that this was just a role he was playing, and his jaw tightened with his resolve to keep up the pretense. Seeing the set of his jaw, Sandra said in a disappointed voice "I can return it if you don't like it." Zack thought quickly, "No, no, it's a great gift, I just hope it didn't set you back too much." Sandra smiled and replied, "You're worth every penny of it, oh, I almost forgot, I had them put an inscription on the back." Zack turned it over and read *To my darling Zachary, love and kisses always, Cassandra.* Sandra then took it from his hands and, as he had done with her, clasped it around his wrist. They sealed the exchange of gifts with a kiss.

***

New Year's Eve in Times Square, it was a moment to remember. Sandra was exhilarated and actually trembling from the thrill of it. She clung to Zack as the excitement of the crowd escalated. As the ball started to drop, the countdown began, "Ten, nine, eight, seven, six, five, four, three, two, one, happy 2008!".

Chapter 4

Veronica Sutton narrowed her eyes, the icy slits shooting daggers at Cassandra. How the hell did she do it? She had nothing, was reduced to a nobody, and yet, there she was with a stupid contented smile on her face. What was it going to take to grind the little bitch down into the ground once and for all?

Cassandra Carrington, Veronica hated that name, just hated it! She could still remember years ago when she had been passed over for a key role that would have made her famous, the role given to little Casey Carrington. Well, no more. Veronica had just secured a leading movie role, and she wasn't going to take the chance that Casandra was going to rise out of the ashes and take away her thunder. No, she had to make sure Cassandra remained down-trodden. She had to strip her of any self-esteem she might be clinging to. The first thing Veronica was going to do was wipe that annoying smile off of Cassandra's face.

***

Sandra was flabbergasted. She was wondering what was up when Mr. Wing, looking sheepish, called her into his office. It must have been difficult for him to approach her on the subject. Actually, he hadn't said a word to her, just handed her the anonymous letter.

Sandra had read it in disbelief. *Dear Mr. Wing, I am a regular patron of your restaurant and feel I must voice my displeasure in regards to one of your waitresses. According to her name tag, her name is Sandra, and I couldn't help but notice how she goes around the restaurant flaunting her body and coming on to the male patrons like, pardon the vulgarity, a bitch in heat. I strongly suggest that you require her to cover herself up as her present mode of dress is making me lose my appetite. I refuse to frequent your restaurant again until this staff member cleans up her act, and I shall also suggest to my friends that they also boycott your establishment until this matter is resolved.*

Sandra left the restaurant feeling physically sick. It was almost too much effort for her to drag herself into her apartment. Once there, she headed straight to the bathroom and threw up. Still upset from the day's events, she found it hard to wind down. She couldn't even vent to Zack because he was out of town on business for a couple of days. He said he had taken a sabbatical in his writing but had gotten an offer that he wanted to look into further, but that meant meeting the people from the magazine in person. She ran herself a hot bath, and immersed her body in the lavender scented water and felt the tension that had built up inside of her drain away.

***

The next morning Sandra awoke determined to be optimistic, but it just wasn't working. She couldn't shake the sick feeling in the pit of her stomach from the day before. Up until now Sandra hadn't missed a day of work, but today she was going to have to call in sick. But, first things first, her number one priority this morning was to make it to the bathroom before she vomited right there in her bed.

***

Pregnant! The nausea Sandra had been feeling left her body and was replaced by shock. Pregnant! But how? She had been diligent about taking her birth control pills. The doctor explained that several things could affect the effectiveness of the pill, like taking antibiotics or not taking the pill in the same time frame each day. Of course, the trip to New York! She always took her pill at breakfast, but breakfast time in New York was not at the same time as breakfast in Los Angeles. It hadn't even crossed her mind to make any adjustments to her routine during that time.

Sandra left the clinic on shaky legs. She was both excited and nervous. She was going to have a baby, Zack's baby! She could barely contain herself, how was she going to keep this news to herself for the next couple of days until he came home? She wondered how this was going to affect their relationship. Would they move in together? Would he tell the news to his parents in Idaho? Would it cause a reconciliation with them?

Zack had told her that his father had practically disowned him when he broke it to his parents that he was moving to Los Angeles. Apparently his father had wanted Zack to stay on the potato farm and take over for him when he retired, but Zack had other plans. Sandra was convinced that the introduction of a grandchild would be the perfect opportunity to end the cold war.

***

During those two days when Sandra was waiting for Zack to return, she did a lot of thinking. She thought mostly about the life that was growing inside her. She had initially been so anxious to tell Zack the news right away, but now she had her doubts. What if he wasn't as happy as she was about having a baby? Should she wait for a bit and feel things out? Maybe she could wait for the subject of kids to come up and then get a better idea of what his thoughts on having children was. Yes, she would wait. In the meantime, this was going to be her little secret. Sandra put one hand on her flat stomach. She was only one month along and wasn't anywhere near showing yet, so she could possibly get away with waiting a couple of more months before she broke the news. With her free hand, Sandra crossed her fingers.

***

Zack called Sandra on the day that he said he was going to return. He really hadn't been out of town like he had led her to believe. He had fabricated the story to keep up the pretense of being a free-lance writer. Although he had told her that he had taken a break from it, he didn't want her to get suspicious if the break from it went on too long. He was finding it harder and harder to keep up the double life he was living, avoiding his friends and family. He was missing his usual haunts, and although he was careful to avoid the places where he was well-known, he knew it would be a matter of time before he ran into someone he knew who would blow his cover.

Zack was lounging on his sofa and put down the magazine he was flipping through. He picked up his cell phone and checked the time. It was just after four o'clock. He had called Sandra the night before, telling her that his flight would be arriving at eight o'clock tonight. She had insisted on meeting him at the airport, but he wasn't feeling up to heading there with a full suitcase and trying to figure out how he could make it look like he had just gotten off of the plane. He called Sandra to tell her that he had managed to get on an earlier flight and was already home, so he would just see her tomorrow.

Sandra was disappointed by Zack's news, but at least, it took the decision out of her hands as to whether or not to tell Zack about the baby right away. She had now firmly decided that she would wait to tell him. After the call had ended, Sandra leaned back and closed her eyes. She caressed her stomach in a circular motion and hummed a lullaby.

***

The next day Zack told Sandra that the business deal had not gone through. He also said that he was going to pursue more writing opportunities eventually, but not in the near future. He figured this would buy him more time before Sandra became suspicious.

Sandra managed not to show it, but she found Zack's news unsettling. She didn't know how established Zack was financially. He always seemed to have money, however, was it running out with him not working? She had never really given it a thought before, but with a baby on the way, it changed things. Right now she was working, but what about once she had the baby? She wouldn't be able to go back to work right away. She really began to worry about what the future held for her and the baby.

***

After Zack's return, Sandra felt that he was slowly withdrawing from her. Was it her imagination? Was she just being insecure? Or, was she just being overly sensitive because her hormones were going crazy? Sandra tried to put the thoughts out of her mind. She didn't want to believe that the relationship was ending, so she hung in there, hoping that things would improve. She tried to concentrate on the positive and the joy and happiness she would feel once the baby was born. Her thoughts turned to names for the baby. If it was a girl, maybe Carolyn after her mother. What if it was a boy? Perhaps her father's name? She never knew her father, and whenever she asked her mother about him, her mother refused to talk about him. The only thing her mother told her about him was his name, Karl. But then again, if it was a boy, perhaps Zack would want the baby to be named after him. She hoped Zack was going to accept the baby and love it as much as she already loved it.

**

It was now two months since Sandra had found out that she was pregnant. She looked at her naked body in the mirror, and she could see a roundness to her belly. She had been reluctant to bring up the subject of children with Zack because in the last couple of months he had seemed somewhat distant, so she still wasn't sure how he would react to the news of a baby. However, now that she was starting to show, she couldn't put it off any longer. She decided that today was going to be the day that she was going to break the news. She got dressed and headed to the doctor's office for her checkup.

**

The checkup went well, and Sandra left the doctor's office full of excitement and a renewed sense of hope for the future. She was wound up and, not wanting to go home to an empty apartment, she wandered up and down the streets, stopping to look in a shop window here and there. Movement in one of the windows caught her eye and what she saw captured her heart. Sad eyes looked through the glass at her and padded paws pressed up against the window pane. What a sweet puppy! She stepped into the shop to get a closer look.

"It's a Doberman," said the sales clerk as he approached Sandra looking at the puppy. Sandra asked, "Aren't they vicious?" The sales clerk explained, "That's just a myth. The reason why some Dobermans are mean is because their owners train them that way. They are actually a very loyal dog, and very protective towards their owners." Protective, she thought, wouldn't it be nice for her child to have such a friend to watch out for him or her?

With the pet carrier in hand, she started for home. She should have had the puppy delivered; he was getting heavier by the minute. It's a good thing that the pet shop wasn't that far from home. Where would home be? Would she give up her apartment to move in with Zack? Did his apartment building allow pets? Or maybe they would decide to move into a house together. Sandra became more excited as she made her way home, looking forward to her future life with Zack and their baby.

***

A baby! Zack couldn't believe what he was hearing. Sandra watched in dismay as Zack went from being the warm, loving man she knew, to an animal, a caged animal. He paced back and forth, not saying a word, but Sandra knew that a lot was going through his mind by watching all of the expressions that crossed his face.

Zack's head was spinning. A baby! It changed everything! It ruined everything! His father had forbidden him to see Cassandra in the first place, and now it was just a matter of time before it would all come out. He would lose his inheritance! He couldn't allow that to happen. He couldn't start from scratch; he was used to a life of luxury, and he wasn't willing to give it up. No, he would not give it up! He had to make a choice and he decided that he would have to end it with Cassandra. But what about the baby? The baby is what stood between him and the inheritance which was rightfully his!

The joy that Sandra had felt when she broke the news to Zack turned to terror. She had never seen this side of him, and it scared her. She found herself backing away, stopping only when she was pressed up against the wall. Then Zack, in one swift move, came face to face with her. His jaw was tense, and Sandra barely heard his words, "Get rid of it!" The words rang in her ears. She closed her eyes, hoping that by doing so she could close out what he had just said. It didn't help; it only prevented her from seeing Zack, who with all of his might, delivered a powerful blow to her stomach. Sandra's eyes opened wide, only to close again as she slid down the wall. She lost consciousness just as Zack walked out the door.

***

Karen knew what it was like when you first entered a relationship. The honeymoon stage where you couldn't bear to be separated from each other for even a minute, but this was ridiculous. In her opinion, it was time for Sandra to come up for some air. Determined, Karen rapped loudly on Sandra's door. There wasn't any welcoming "Come in", just a low moan coming from inside the apartment. Karen tried the door, and it was unlocked, so she let herself in. Inside she saw Sandra, half-conscious on the floor, a floor covered in blood where Sandra was laying. Karen grabbed her cell phone and called 911. She quickly gave the information needed, all the while staying by Sandra's side.

Karen asked, "Sandra, are you alright? What happened?" All Sandra could muster was a low moan and a faint plea, "My baby, don't let me lose my baby." Karen was shocked. Obviously, a great deal had happened since the last time she had talked with Sandra. Karen told Sandra not to speak, to save her energy, and then she made Sandra as comfortable as possible.

The sound of the siren was music to Karen's ears. She briefly left Sandra to run down the flight of stairs and onto the street where she flagged down the ambulance and led the paramedics to Sandra's apartment. They worked swiftly, and it wasn't long before Sandra was inside the ambulance and on her way to the hospital.

Karen watched the ambulance head off into the distance. Only then did she let herself breathe a sigh of relief. She returned to Sandra's apartment and proceeded to wash the blood off of the floor. Her long, curly brown hair almost brushed the floor as she continued to scrub, her lean athletic body attacking the stain with vigour. It wasn't until she had just finished cleaning up the last bit of blood that she felt eyes upon her. Still on her hands and knees, she turned her head to one side and demanded, "And what exactly am I supposed to do with you?" The only response she received was a whimper and a cold nose pressed up against hers. Brown eyes looked into brown eyes. Karen stretched and got up from the floor. She scooped the puppy up in one arm, and with the other closed the door to Sandra's apartment. She reached up and got the spare key from on top of the door frame and locked the door. The puppy squirmed and let out a yelp. Karen said in a scolding tone, "Oh shush, for now, you're stuck with me whether you like it or not, and it works both ways I might add." With those words, Karen held the puppy even tighter as she fumbled with the keys to her own apartment.

***

The group of nurses met in the hospital staff lounge as they did most days. There was usually four of them but one of them, Karen, had recently been switched to a different schedule. Barbara was a tall, buxom brunette who had no problem expressing what was on her mind. She went after what she wanted and many a time had managed to extract invitations to high-profile parties from some of the doctors at the hospital and also from some of the celebrity patients. Jen, a short, petite blonde with a short pixie haircut slowly made her way into the staff room, her face turning red in embarrassment when Barbara blurted out, "So out with it Jen, how did it go last night?" Noticing Jen's red face, Barbara turned to Vera and said, "Oh, it's gotta be good, look at how red she's turning!" Barbara and Vera exchanged devilish looks. Vera was of medium height with an hourglass figure and pale long, blonde hair. She could be just as outspoken as Barbara. Both Vera and Barbara turned to Jen, arms folded and Vera spoke for the both of them, "Okay, spill it, Jen." Jen retorted, "If you're talking about my so-called date, I ended it early." Barbara replied, "But you've wanted to date James for so long, ever since he started at the hospital six months ago." Vera added, "And ever since you started going out with him about a month ago you've been inseparable. Why have things changed?" Jen turned red all over again, "Well, I wanted to take it all the way, but when we got on the subject of sex, well..." "Come on, don't stop now." Vera coaxed. Jen continued, "...well, it sounds like he wants to, well, not exactly enter me by, uh, the conventional way." Barbara squealed, "You mean he wants to enter by the back door?" Jen nodded. Vera piped in, "Let me guess, and you've never done that before?" Jen was hesitant, "No, have you?" Vera replied, "Oh sure, piece of cake." Vera thought for a moment then continued, "You know, you really have to wonder about a guy who would prefer that over conventional intercourse. How do you know a guy isn't secretly wishing he was doing it with another man instead of with you?" Barbara retorted, "Oh thanks for that thought, now whenever I find myself in that situation, I'm going to wonder about that, thanks for ruining it for me!" Vera defended, "Well, you do have to wonder." Barbara then turned to Jen, "Okay Jen, this is the game plan. If he brings up the subject, here's how you'll handle it. Got a vibrator?" Jen shook her head. Barbara continued, "Well get yourself one, a *big* one, and if he says that he wants to do it that way, tell him okay, but you want to do it to him first, and then pull out the *big* one!" Jen couldn't help but laugh, "Oh Barbara, you're so bad! But what do I do if he doesn't want to, but still wants to do it to me?" Barbara thought for a moment, felt around in her pocket, pulled out a scrap of paper and pen then wrote down a name and phone number. She handed the piece of paper to Jen and said, "Well, if you really don't want to do it anally, then, you can hand him this name and number of a gay friend of mine and tell him that it's the number of a guy who would love to oblige him." Jen was mortified, "I couldn't, I wouldn't have the nerve!" Barbara replied, "Well, keep it just in case, you just never know." Then all three women got up and left the room, each going their separate ways down the corridors of the hospital.

***

The two police officers had left the patient's hospital room in frustration. The young woman had been despondent and refused to talk, keeping her face and body turned towards the one wall. As they got back into the police cruiser, Office Jones thought to herself why, oh why were so many women that were victims of domestic abuse unwilling to press charges? This case was extra frustrating as the woman refused to even give them her boyfriend's name. She made herself a note to follow up with the woman after she left the hospital. Maybe by then she will have had a change of heart.

* * *

Vera walked into the hospital room where the only occupant was a very pale young woman. Careful not to wake her, she walked quietly to the foot of the bed and looked at the chart. How sad, a miscarriage. She had heard about this case that had come in earlier that day. Apparently the miscarriage had been caused by a severe blow to the abdomen. How could anybody be so cruel? Vera noticed the patient stirring and went to her side, "Hi, how are you feeling?" Sandra's only reply was a single tear running down her cheek. Vera said encouragingly, "Oh hon, I'm so sorry, but you're young, you're sure to have more babies." Sandra turned her face away, "I... I don't think I could ever be with another man, ever!" Vera replied, "You shouldn't think that way dear, there are plenty of men out there, you've just got to find the right kind. Men are like bras if they don't offer some form of support, why bother with them?" Sandra couldn't help but smile at that, and Vera went on to say, "Ah, that's better, I'll just go get you something to drink, did you want water or juice?" Sandra answered, "Water please." Vera replied, "Good, I'll be back in a moment, and remember what I said about men, and beware of those sexy, flimsy ones, they may look good at first, but eventually they're going to let you down." and with that Vera turned to go. Sandra gave another weak smile, but it quickly vanished once Vera left the room.

***

Since first being admitted to the hospital Sandra's emotions had constantly changed as the events that had happened replayed again and again in her mind. She mourned for her lost child. They told her that it had been a boy. She felt sadness and emptiness at the thought of a childless future, and then she felt betrayed. Betrayed by the one she had loved. That last one cut like a knife and hurt more than any physical pain she had felt throughout the entire ordeal. But now, now she became angry, angry at the man who took the life from inside of her. It was her body; it should have been her choice whether or not to keep the baby, even if he wouldn't have wanted anything to do with it. How dared he!

Vera returned with the water and noted, "Well you must be feeling a little better, you've got some colour in your face, here, drink up." Sandra took the glass but didn't drink right away; she asked tentatively, "What... what do they... do with..." "With the fetus?" Vera finished. Sandra nodded. Vera asked, "Oh hon, did you want to take it with you? Have a little memorial ceremony for it?" Sandra became overcome with emotion and could barely nod her head. Vera said comfortingly, "You just hold on dear, I'll see what I can do, okay?" Vera left the room and headed down the corridor to the elevator and pressed the button for the basement.

Vera stepped out of the elevator into the basement then headed to the morgue. She found out that Clara, the nurse that had been working in the emergency room when Sandra had been admitted, had taken the fetus and put it in an empty jar that she had found in a supply room. Clara had labeled the jar and taken it to the hospital morgue where she had handed it over to the coroner to store until it was found out if Sandra wanted it or not.

Vera asked the coroner on duty to search for the fetus. He found it and handed the jar to Vera. Vera took a look at the contents of the jar. She couldn't very well give it to Sandra like that. She headed to a supply room and scanned the shelves that held some supplies, ah, there! She reached up to the top shelf and took down a roll of gauze. She wound the gauze around the jar until the fetus within it was hidden.

Vera returned to Sandra's room just as another nurse was helping Sandra into a wheelchair. It was time for Sandra to go home. Vera didn't go into the room, but instead headed towards the exit. She waiting until Sandra was settled into a waiting taxi, then rushed up to the taxi just before it left. The window was open and, without a word, Vera handed the jar to Sandra. Sandra took it and mouthed a "thank you" as the taxi pulled away.

Sandra clutched the jar, feeling guilty. She had misled the nurse into thinking that she wanted the fetus for a memorial ceremony, but she had other plans. The bitterness welled up inside of her as she took the note she had written while waiting for the nurse to return with the fetus. She didn't have any tape to attach the note to the jar, so she tucked the note partway under the gauze that was wrapped tightly around the jar. The taxi came to a stop, and Sandra instructed the driver to wait for her. Her movements were slow as she made her way to her destination. She entered the apartment building and placed the jar in front of the apartment door, then returned to the taxi. She fell back onto the seat in the taxi, then gave the driver the address to her own apartment.

***

Damn it! Zack threw another book into the box. He had been packing his stuff up ever since he had gotten back to his apartment. It was over! The damn bitch had ruined everything by getting pregnant! He had to remove all traces of ever being here, or ever knowing her! He had to make sure that his father never found out about the relationship so that he could keep his inheritance intact. He had counted on his father's money ever since he had been a young boy and there was no way he was giving it up. He closed up the last of the boxes just as the moving van pulled up. It wasn't easy getting one on such short notice, but cold hard cash talks. He opened the door to let the movers in and almost kicked over the small object at his feet. He picked it up and put it on the window sill. He would deal with it later, right now he had to get the hell out of there.

***

Sandra read the note that was taped to the door of her apartment; *The puppy is with me, come over and talk*. It was signed *Karen*. The tears welled up in Sandra's eyes. Karen was becoming such a good friend, but she really felt like she needed time just to herself. She knocked softly on Karen's door, and it opened almost immediately. Karen took one look at Sandra's face and knew the worst. Karen embraced Sandra, and Sandra's tears started to flow. Karen said, "I can understand that you don't want to talk right now, but when you do, you know where to find me. But you have to do me a favour." Karen stooped down and picked up the puppy, "You have to take him back now! He's done nothing but whine the whole time you were gone!" Sandra took the puppy and hugged it to her. It responded by licking her face. Sandra thought to herself that he just might be the therapy she needed.

***

Zack leaned on the window sill. He was exhausted, but it was well worth the effort, all of the furniture was gone along with any trace that he had ever been there. He moved to leave, almost knocking over the jar with his elbow. He had forgotten all about it, but now he picked it up and studied it. How odd. He pulled the note out from under the gauze and started to read. He then opened the jar and barely made it to the bathroom before he threw up.

***

Rage. It took over his body and mind, the words of the note echoing in his head, *I didn't want your child either, here it is!* The words cut like a knife. So, his kid wasn't good enough for her. The bitch! The whore! Who did she think she was, rejecting him, rejecting his flesh and blood! He'd show her!

***

Sandra was floating on a large puffy white cloud high in the sky. It was swirling, circling a smaller cloud. On that cloud was a sweet, happy baby, gurgling and squealing with delight. The clouds came together, and as Sandra went to reach out to the child, the cloud gave way and the baby started to fall towards the earth, except it wasn't the earth as she knew it, it was a ball of fire. The baby's delight turned to terror and its screams haunted Sandra. She could bear it no longer and leaped off of her cloud, her body plummeting towards the fiery hell. Sandra awoke with a start, but her nightmare didn't end there, it had just begun. Towering over her was Zack. She screamed in terror as the knife ripped open her flesh.

Chapter 5

Toma Kato's hands shook as he held her picture. It was his favourite, taken shortly after their first wedding anniversary. They had been having a picnic in the park, her sundress was flared out around her on the blanket, and the camera captured her image just as she had been delightfully surprised by a passing butterfly. He never got tired of looking at her upturned face, the angle showing to the best advantage her beautiful bone structure. But that wasn't the full extent of her beauty. It came from within and shone through from her smiling eyes.

They had spent many happy years together since that time. Toma thought back to when he had met Mika. Although Toma had been born and raised in the United States, his parents had both come over from Japan. They tried to fit in as best they could, adopting most American customs, but still hung on to some traditions. They firmly believed in arranged marriages and had promised him to the daughter of a couple they had known well in Japan. Toma was all set to defy them. He had refused to greet his bride-to-be at the airport but was finally tricked into meeting her at a restaurant. The moment he had laid eyes on Mika, all resistance faded away. When their eyes met, they both knew they had found their soul mate.

Years passed, and their love grew. Their only regret was that they had never had children. For years, Mika had subjected herself to clinical tests, but to no avail. It was finally discovered that the problem was not with Mika, but with Toma. But by that time, it was too late. Mika was diagnosed with cancer of the uterus. She had fought the battle and won but did not come out of it unscathed. The experience made them realize one thing; they had each other, and that was enough. They began living life to its fullest and did so for many years until it struck again. Cancer had invaded Mika's left breast and spread quickly. This time, she would not be saved.

It was almost two years ago now since Mika's passing, but Toma's pain had not dulled with time. He was about to go further down into his despair when the ringing of the phone jarred him out of it. Still in a bit of a daze, he answered the phone. It was the police. Toma was even more dazed after the phone call. He grabbed his car keys and was on his way to the building he owned on Wilshire Boulevard. When the police said there was in incident in his building, he immediately thought there must have been a fire in the Chinese restaurant that Mr. Wing leased. But it wasn't a fire, and it wasn't in the restaurant, it was an attempted murder in one of the apartments above.

***

Toma pulled into the back lane of his building and ran up the back stairs to the second story where the apartments were. He headed down the hallway where police officers were at the open doorway of the apartment. He answered Officer Jones' questions as best he could, but he had to admit that aside from the victim's name and age, he didn't know anything about the young woman. He caught a glimpse through the open doorway through to the bedroom and was sickened by the scene; blood was everywhere including on the blood-soaked bed. What kind of person could have done all this? What kind of savage would do such a heinous thing to another human being?

He heard what sounded like a faint whimper coming from the bathroom just as an officer came through the bathroom door carrying a shivering puppy. The officer said, "Look what I found, it was cowering behind the bathroom door. I noticed a buckled dog collar hanging from the hook on the back of the door. Judging by the blood on this little guy I'd say the perpetrator may have actually hung him on the hook by his collar. Luckily the collar must have been loose enough that he slipped through it and fell to the floor. Too bad he can't talk, he's probably the only eye witness we have." "Well bag the collar, there may be prints on it, but first, figure out what to do with him," said a second officer as he pointed towards the puppy. Toma looked at the furry bundle in the officer's arms and impulsively offered "I'll take him." The officer was visibly relieved and walked to the doorway and handed the puppy over to him. The officer then went back into the bathroom to retrieve and bag the collar.

Toma turned back to Officer Jones and asked some questions of his own. How was the woman? Was she still alive? Had they taken her to a hospital yet, and if so, which one? The officer told him that she was in critical condition, she had lost a lot of blood, and that she was already on her way to the hospital. Toma got the name of the hospital and asked if he could be excused. He knew he wasn't responsible in any way for what had happened, but he still felt compelled to go to the hospital and check on the woman himself. With puppy in tow, Toma was on his way. Officer Jones watched him go. It was a miracle that dog survived. She just hoped that Sandra was going to be just as lucky.

Officer Jones was frustrated. She hadn't been able to get Sandra to open up at the hospital, and she had been hoping that, by doing a follow-up visit to Sandra at home, she could get her to open up to her, woman to woman. She certainly hadn't expected to find what she had but had a sinking feeling the moment that she had seen that the apartment door had been left ajar. She had been further frustrated knowing that, had she shown up even ten minutes earlier than she had, that she could have caught the bastard, or better yet, prevented this horrible crime altogether.

***

Barbara said to Vera as Jen entered the staff room, "Shh! Here she comes." They watched Jen as she pulled a chair up to the table and sat down heavily. Both Barbara and Vera said in unison, "Well?" Jen stayed silent. Vera guessed, "I take it your date with James didn't go so well?" Jen folded her arms on the table and put her head down on them, "I feel so humiliated!" Barbara asked, "What happened that was so bad? Did you take my advice?" Jen managed to get out, "I did everything you said, and..." "And?" Barbara prompted. Jen raised her head and continued hesitantly, "First I suggested, you know, about the vibrator and he should go first and... and he wasn't sure, and then I brought up the number of that gay guy Troy, and..." Vera demanded, "Come on, don't stop there!" Jen continued, "And, he... he took Troy's number and left!" and with that outburst, Jen crossed her arms across her chest and pouted.

Vera and Barbara both burst into laughter. Vera apologized, "I'm sorry Jen, but the look on your face, and you have to admit, this just confirms what we're always telling you, when it comes to your love life, you're jinxed!" Jen was defensive, "How can you say that?" Vera retorted, "Oh come on, a few months ago you went out with that loser who got drunk and dropped his pants, and a couple of months before that, it was the guy who, at the end of your first and only date, told you to take your clothes off." Barbara kidded, "Ya, the guy was even too lazy to take them off himself." Vera looked at her watch and said with a sigh, "Well, time to get back to it." She wasn't prepared for what was to come next.

***

It was chaos. When the ambulance pulled up at the emergency room entrance, the paramedics were still trying to stabilize the patient. The emergency room team took over. Vera was part of that team, and although she prided herself on being able to handle anything, the sight of the person on the operating table made her feel faint. Was it a man or woman? She couldn't even tell at this point; it was hard to make out anything distinguishable, the person was just one bloody mass.

The bleeding was finally stopped. The patient was finally stabilized and in intensive care. It was time for all of them to go home. Vera was exhausted, but she wanted to do one final thing. Out of curiosity, she looked at the name on the patient's chart. Why was that name so familiar? Wasn't it just the other day that she had seen that name before? Then it hit her that it was the woman who had just lost her baby, the one that she had given the jar to in the taxi as she was leaving the hospital. Who would have thought that the woman's situation would escalate to this!

The nurse in the waiting area walked up and gently nudged Toma's shoulder. He awoke with a start. The nurse announced, "She is fine for now." and Toma let out a sigh of relief. He wasn't sure why he was taking this whole thing so personally; he just felt that he needed to do something. That was why he had decided to take it upon himself to cover the costs of the woman's medical bills. After all, he had more money than he could ever use up in his lifetime. He had amassed quite a fortune throughout the years, throwing himself into his work, trying to fill the empty spot that children would have filled. He eventually invested in real estate and had acquired quite an empire. But it meant nothing to him, money couldn't bring back his Mika.

***

Karen received the news and collapsed onto the sofa. She was so relieved that Sandra was hanging in there. She still couldn't get the horrible image out of her mind. Being a nurse she thought that the sight of blood wouldn't have bothered her, but it was different when it was someone you knew. It made it personal. And such a violent act. Karen shuddered. How could someone be capable of such violence? She couldn't even begin to comprehend. She had just been returning from her shift from the hospital and arrived home just as they were rushing Sandra out of her apartment. Well, she had assumed it was Sandra because it was Sandra's apartment, but the blood and the wounds made it impossible to tell.

Karen thought of all the questions the police had asked her. She felt guilty that she couldn't have been more helpful. It made her realize how little she knew about what was going on in her friend's life. They had asked her if Sandra had a boyfriend, what his name was, where he lived and worked, could she give them a description of him, were Sandra and her boyfriend getting along okay, and the questions went on and on. The only information that Karen could impart was his name, Zack Dungess and a vague description of what he looked like, based on how Sandra had described him to her on one occasion.

***

Right away the police made inquiries to get any information they could on Zachary, aka Zack Dungess, but they drew a blank. It was as if the man didn't exist. They were going to have to hang tight on this one; the victim wasn't going to be able to fill them in anytime soon. In the meantime, they weren't sure if she was still in danger from her attacker. The decision was made to release to the press that an unidentified woman had passed away from her injuries. It was best the attacker thought her dead and that he had succeeded in his sad, twisted mission.

***

Karen was torn. Should she go on the trip she had planned or be by her friend's side? She weighed both sides and finally decided to follow through on her original plan. She had committed herself to this six-month tour of Europe almost a year ago when she had gotten in touch with Kate, a childhood friend. They had talked for hours and had decided on this trip. Now Kate was already on her way from New Jersey, and Karen felt that she couldn't back out at this point in time. Her mind made up, Karen further tried to justify her decision, she had already taken the leave of absence from work, and there wasn't anything she could do for Sandra that the capable medical staff at the hospital weren't already doing. She packed some last minute items into her already too full suitcases.

***

Dr. Whitford looked grim as he sat down with Toma. Although Sandra was out of immediate danger, there had been a lot of damage done, and she was still in critical condition. The doctor went on to say that they had to remove her spleen. They were able to keep her reproductive system intact, but it she were to get pregnant in the future, it was questionable if she would be able to carry to term. It had been a miracle in itself that no critical organs were destroyed, but then again, most of the knife wounds weren't that deep. It seemed that the attacker wasn't so much intent on stabbing as he had been on slashing almost every part of her body and face.

The doctor cleared his throat. It was never easy speaking to the family members, especially on the subject of money. This was even more awkward as the man paying Sandra's medical bills wasn't even a relative, and what he had understood from what he had heard, Sandra and this man in front of him had never even met. It would be interesting to see whether Mr. Kato would bail once he realized just how much he had taken on financially.

Dr. Witford told it straight. He said that Sandra was going to need care for a long time. Once her internal injuries were healed to his satisfaction, he would concentrate on the reconstruction of her face and her body. Sandra's assailant had done quite a number on her, and there would have to be extensive cosmetic work done. He went on to explain that Toma was looking at the costs of the surgeries, but also the expense of a lengthy hospital stay. It was hard to pinpoint a particular dollar amount, so he could only give a rough estimate of the costs involved. He took a deep breath and quoted a rather phenomenal sum, then looked closely at Toma for his reaction. To his surprise, Toma didn't even bat an eye, he simply nodded his head in acceptance.

It was a done deal then. Dr. Whitford went into a more detailed account and then escorted Toma to the door. Just as Toma was leaving, the doctor stopped him and said, "Oh, one other thing. The damage to Sandra's face was quite extensive, and there's not much for us to go on. Would you be able to provide a picture of her for the surgeon to use as a guideline?" Toma thought only for a moment before reaching for his wallet. He pulled out the well-worn photograph, took one last loving look at it and then hesitantly held it out to the doctor. The doctor took it gently from his hand. After Toma had left, Dr. Whitford looked at the photograph and the beautiful woman with the smiling eyes.

* * *

The female attendant behind the airline counter looked at the man who had come up to the counter and said to him, "Your passport please." Fraser Douglas handed his passport over and looked casually around as the attendant studied it. The attendant took longer than usual to look at the photo on the passport. She couldn't help but think that Mr. Douglas was an exceptionally attractive man. "Mr. Douglas," she said to get his attention. He swiveled around, pushing a hand through his silvery blonde hair. "You can board now," she advised. He thanked her, flashing her a charming smile, and headed towards the airplane bound for the French Riviera. He settled into first class and flagged down a flight attendant. Ah, he thought to himself, this was the only way to fly, and the perfect time to get away.

Once in the air, Fraser felt he could, at last, breathe a sigh of relief. He had released all of his anger and had regained control of his emotions. He had always had a volatile temper, never very far from the surface, but never had he totally lost control like that, to actually brutally murder someone! He had never thought himself capable of such a thing. That is until he had met *her*. But then, she had gotten to him in so many ways that no other woman ever had. Well never again! He was heading to the French Riviera not only to get away until he was sure the situation had blown over at home but also to have a carefree time. He was going to have a time to remember, in order to forget.

His left hand touched the cold metal of his Rolex. He looked down at his other wrist and at the ID bracelet on it. He turned the bracelet over so that he could read the inscription on the back, *To my darling Zachary, love and kisses always, Cassandra.* It was the last piece of evidence that could link him to Cassandra, what better place to get rid of it than another country?

***

Veronica stood in the doorway of the restaurant and looked around, wondering where the little twit was. This was her third visit to the restaurant in a month and each time there was no sign of Ms. Carrington. Well, her ploy to defeat Cassandra had gone maybe a little too well. Veronica had set out to make her life miserable, but she hadn't planned on Cassandra actually quitting her job over it. Now how was she going to keep an eye on the bitch if she didn't know where she was? Veronica shrugged as she thought that maybe Ms. Carrington couldn't have been much of a threat to her in the first place. Veronica turned to Chelsea and said, "You know, I think I've tired of this place, let's try somewhere new." Chelsea agreed and they walked back out the door.

***

Toma looked outside. He surveyed the yard, taking in the fruit trees in bloom to the left and the brilliantly coloured flower garden to the right. Summer was here. The time had flown, and now he decided there was no more putting it off. He was going to have to go to Sandra's apartment and pack up her possessions and bring them here. As Sandra was going to need care after her release from the hospital, he decided that she would be better off in his home. Besides, how would she feel going back to the apartment, he didn't even want to go back there himself. He picked up the phone and called his office. He instructed his secretary to hire a moving company to move everything from the apartment to his home. Once the apartment was empty, it was to remain empty. No one else was ever to live in that suite again.

That done, Toma went back to the window. He smiled as he watched the gangly half-pup, half-dog tearing through the yard. One time when he took him to the vet, the vet had suggested to Toma that he might want to have the dog's ears pinned back. So now, here was the dog in his back yard, with what looked like empty toilet paper rolls on his head. The dog jumped up into the air time and time again trying to catch the odd butterfly that fluttered by, blissfully unaware of how comical he looked. Toma couldn't help but think that maybe Brutus, the name he had picked for the dog, wasn't a very good choice. It didn't suit this playful, friendly dog, a far cry from the cowering, distrustful pup he had taken home that fateful day. But who could blame the poor thing, after being hung up on a coat hook, left to hang to death. It made Toma angry every time he thought about it.

***

Pain. All she could think of was the pain. It hurt to move a muscle. It hurt to blink. Vera was adjusting Sandra's sheets when she heard the moan. She was finally coming out of what was to be the last of many surgeries. Vera rushed out of the room to find Dr. Whitford.

Dr. Whitford hurried to Sandra's room. He wanted to be there when she came to. Although she had been conscious for short times between each surgery, he had felt it best to keep her in induced comas and sedated throughout most of her ordeal. Otherwise, the pain would have been unbearable, and he was also concerned about any mental anguish she may be suffering. But now, there would be no more heavy sedation, and she was going to have a lot of questions. He wanted to have a chance to talk to her and explain what had been going on. He knew he wouldn't have much time before the police came and started to question her.

***

It all came flooding back to her. The pregnancy, the blow to her stomach, the jar and the note, all leading up to her awakening to find Zack standing over her. The disbelief she had felt, the disbelief she still felt. And the pain! How could he have done this to her?

***

She turned her head slightly when a tall, gray-haired man wearing a white coat came into her room. He introduced himself as Dr. Whiford and sat down in a chair beside her bed. He explained to her the various surgeries she had undergone, the damage that had been done, and what she could expect while recovering from her cosmetic surgery. Sandra listened to it all, her body becoming very tense. Again she had to ask herself, how could he have done this to her. He had all but left her for dead! He had almost murdered her!

Dr. Whitford mistook her reaction and said, "Don't worry, Toma Kato has taken care of all your medical expenses. Sandra thought, who? What? She didn't know any Toma Kato. What did he have to do with her? How did he know her? And why was he taking it upon himself to pay her hospital bills? She opened her mouth to speak, but the pain in her jaw stopped her. The doctor, seeing her agitation, recommended that she rest. He ordered the nurse to administer a mild sedative. Sandra fell into a deep sleep, a temporary freedom from the pain.

It was like a hurricane had come through Toma's home, leaving chaos in its wake. Odds and ends of furniture were scattered about, the only semblance of order was the stack of cardboard boxes in one corner of the large entrance way. In hindsight, he should have delegated a specific room for the movers to unload the furniture in, now he was stuck with the task himself.

In the end, Toma ended up using three separate rooms for Sandra's belongings. Her bedroom contained her chest of drawers and vanity. One thing that was not there was the blood-soaked bed. Toma had purchased a new bed to replace it. The room adjacent to her bedroom held her living room furniture. He wasn't sure how much she would want her privacy, but that room would give her the choice of retreating to her own space if she so wished. The third room was just across the hallway and held the extra furniture like her dining room set and stacks of packed boxes.

Toma was relieved to see that there were just a few boxes left to stack. At age fifty-five he felt he was just getting too old for such intense physical activity. He must have been more tired than he thought because as he grabbed another box, it slipped out of his hand and fell to the floor, spilling the contents everywhere. He got down on his hands and knees and began picking up the envelopes and photographs. He noticed the envelopes each held a card. Curious, he pulled one of the cards out of its envelope and started to read, *Thinking of you during your time of sorrow, your mother was a wonderful woman and will be dearly missed.*

He quickly glanced at a few more cards, all expressing sympathy. Poor Sandra, it seemed she had lost her mother, and by the postscripts, it looked like it was only about a year ago.

Then Toma noticed the photographs. He paled as he realized who the person was looking at him from the photos. He knew this face. He had seen it on television and on the theatre screen. Little Casey Carrington. Of course! Her last name was Carrington! Sandra, short for Cassandra. But what had she been doing living in one of his apartments? It just didn't make sense.

Then a thought hit him. Her face! By giving the doctor a picture of his beloved Mika, he had changed her face forever! The face that millions of her fans knew and loved! She was going to be devastated! How could he have played God like that? And once he really thought about it, even if she wasn't famous and didn't have the kind of face found on any movie screen, how would she feel, waking up to have a perfect stranger looking back her in the mirror?

Toma felt sick with shame. Could he ever make it up to her? He would have to, some way, somehow, or he just wouldn't be able to live with himself.

Chapter 6

Sandra was in shock. Didn't exist! That was impossible! Zack Dungess was a living breathing man. A very dangerous one as it had turned out. Officer Jones apologized, "Sorry, but we came up empty, there was nobody by that name living at that address. The owner of the building did say that he had rented it out to a Mr. Dungess, but he always paid his rent in cash, and then one day he cleared out without any notice. We checked your phone records, but it turns out that he was using a burner phone, so there is no way to trace him that way. It seems we've come to a dead end."

Sandra looked worried. "Don't worry," Officer Jones soothed, "it's unlikely that he'll come back for you, we managed to keep your case "hush-hush". There was a very brief story we fed to the newspaper stating that you were an unidentified woman that had been stabbed to death in a domestic dispute. We hope you don't mind that we fabricated your demise, but we didn't know if your assailant would try to come after you again." Sandra thought she was going to be sick. Officer Jones tried to be encouraging, "We're doing all we can to find this guy. Try to concentrate, can you think of anything that could help us track him down?" Sandra shook her head. Officer Jones questioned, "How about the magazines that he had done freelance writing for?" Again, a negative response from Sandra.

After the officer had left the hospital room, Sandra laid back against the pillows. She felt so frustrated and so stupid. How could she have allowed herself to be so gullible? Dr. Whitford walked into the room followed by a short, stocky Asian man. She couldn't help but notice that the man seemed extremely nervous. She looked back towards the doctor.

Dr. Whitford broke the silence, "Sandra, as I understand it, you haven't met Mr. Kato. Sandra, Mr. Toma Kato. Toma, Miss Sandra Carrington." Toma nervously extended his hand, and Sandra managed to extend her still bandaged hand. Toma, realizing her dilemma, took her hand in both of his, giving it a light squeeze. The doctor decided this was as good a time as any to leave.

Both Sandra and Toma were extremely uncomfortable with the situation, and neither knew what to say to break the silence that was growing with each passing minute. Sandra finally spoke. "I don't..." her voice cracked, and she had to clear her throat before continuing, "I don't know how to thank you for all that you've done, paying my hospital bills, your offer for me to stay in your home, it is all so generous of you." The words of thanks made Toma feel extremely uncomfortable. How was she going to feel about his so-called acts of kindness once she was finally able to see the results of her cosmetic surgery? Sandra felt compelled to go on to say that she fully intended to pay him back every cent as soon as she was able to. Toma, hearing the determination in her voice, believed that she would. Being repaid the money was of no consequence to him, but he could see that it was important to her. If the situation were reversed, he would feel the same way.

So Toma agreed to the arrangement but refused to go into any set agreement. There would be plenty of time to work out the details later he told her. He then went on to tell her about himself, who he was, that he owned the building she had been living in, and how he came to be involved in her life. He could see that his words had answered a lot of the questions that she had, but also noticed that she was tired of the way her body was slumped over. He suggested that she should rest for now and he would see her in a couple of days when she was to be released from the hospital. They parted company, both feeling somewhat better about the odd situation they found themselves in.

***

Everything was all set for Sandra's arrival and the arrival of the private nurse he had hired for her. He was just about to take a much-deserved break when he caught a glimpse of his image in a mirror. The mirrors! He hastily went from room to room taking down every mirror he had. He left one in his bedroom and one in the nurse's bedroom as well. He dragged all the rest into a storage room towards the back of the house just off of the kitchen. As he was shutting the door to the storage room, he noticed that he had somehow managed to get some grease on his hands.

Back in his bathroom, as Toma was washing his hands, he looked up, then hung his head in defeat. The medicine cabinet mirrors, he had forgotten all about them. Toma dried his hands and then made a phone call. Within a few hours, all of the medicine cabinets were replaced with ones without mirrors. Money really did talk. Toma collapsed into a nearby chair and put his head in his hands. This was getting way too complicated.

***

Sandra had one large knot in her stomach. She took in her surroundings. The hospital was frequented by the rich and famous and one could tell that extra effort had been put into the design of it to make it look less clinical and more like a spa, but it still fell short for Sandra. To her, it still felt like a hospital. Her body gave an involuntary shudder. As nervous as Sandra was, she was glad to be finally leaving this place. Not that she had anything against the staff, they had all been wonderful, it was just that this place held too many bad memories. Memories of pain, of surgery after surgery, of grueling sessions of physiotherapy. Even now she was still recuperating. She lifted a hand to her face and felt the bandages that still held her bondage. The doctor had assured her that they would be taken off in a couple of weeks. He also warned her not to expect instant results. She sat in the wheelchair that the nurse was waiting beside and didn't look back as she was wheeled away.

Sandra turned as the automatic doors opened. She recognized Mr. Kato and greeted him with a wave of her hand. He said his car was outside and asked if she was ready to go. Sandra replied that she was more than ready, and her nervousness left her as excitement took over. She was so happy to be out of there!

The nurse wheeled her out the door to the waiting black Mercedes. Toma, holding the door handle, turned to Sandra and said, "I hope you don't mind, but I took the liberty of bringing someone along." He opened the door and a bundle of energy bound out of the car. Sandra squealed in delight. Her puppy! Well, he was more of a dog now. She had hardly thought about the puppy; she had assumed that at the time of her hospitalization he had been dropped off at an animal shelter. But here he was, head on her lap, looking up at her with warm brown eyes. She was surprised that he even remembered her. It warmed her heart.

The journey to Toma's house went quickly. Before Sandra knew it, they were passing through tall gates and down a tree lined driveway. The car pulled up in front of a white house; its lines were simple and elegant. Sandra thought that the front pillars gave it a stately presence. Toma got out of the car and opened the back door. The dog bounded out and then Toma offered his arm, which Sandra was grateful for. The muscles in her legs still need to be built up, although, Sandra thought, they probably would have felt weak anyhow under the circumstances.

Just outside the double front doors, three women stood. Toma made the introductions. The first was the cook, Mrs. Emma White, a short, rather plump woman in her mid-fifties. In stark contrast was the housekeeper, Ms. Joan Easton, a tall, almost stick-like figure. Sandra judged her to be about fifty. The third woman was also quite tall, but with a muscular build. She was introduced to Sandra as Ms. Wanda Stock, her private nurse. She was quite a bit younger than the other two, maybe in her early forties. Toma explained that the cook and housekeeper were there during the day only, but that Ms. Stock had agreed to stay in his home and provide her with 24-hour care. There would also be a second nurse coming in on the weekends to allow Wanda time off. Sandra felt relieved by the news, but also discomfort. It made her think of the inconvenience and expense she was causing her host. It just increased the amount of debt she already owed this man.

***

Charlotte Douglas unfolded the newspaper clipping. It was about six months old now, but she kept rereading it. It was like a bad accident; she couldn't help but look. It had an obscure little heading for such a tragic ending to the life of one so young. *Woman Dies in Domestic Dispute* it read. She read on: *Yesterday evening an unidentified woman in her late teens to early twenties was stabbed to death in her rental apartment. The police are considering the stabbing to be an escalation of a domestic dispute. Another victim at the scene was a Doberman puppy who survived and has since been adopted.*

That was it, the end of the story. But deep down inside, Charlotte knew there was more to it than that. Judging by the quick departure of her son out of the country with only a brief, strained message on the answering machine, she kept coming to the conclusion that the young woman was Cassandra Carrington, and the assailant, her son Fraser. She felt a sense of guilt. How could she think such a thing of her own flesh and blood? Her only son? Yet, there was that nagging feeling in her gut that wouldn't let her be. All she could do was wait, wait for her son to return home. Then she would get some answers.

***

Karen couldn't remember the last time she felt so relaxed. She sat back and almost melted into the back seat of the taxi. That vacation was just what the doctor had ordered. She dug her wallet out of her purse as the taxi pulled up to the building. The driver popped the trunk then got out and proceeded to unload what seemed to be an endless supply of suitcases. Not only had Karen brought several months of clothing with her, but her purchases on the trip had accumulated to almost the same amount. She winced at the thought of her charge card bill.

The driver helped her bring the suitcases up the fight of stairs and Karen gave him another tip for the extra service. She turned the key in the lock and her mood suddenly sobered as she glanced towards Sandra's apartment. It was late at night so she wouldn't knock on her door right now. There would be plenty of time for that tomorrow she thought, but first, sleep! Karen took off her clothes and went to bed. The suitcases remained unpacked.

***

The next day Karen began to worry when there wasn't any answer at Sandra's door. Could she still be in the hospital? She phoned the hospital but they must have hired new administrative staff while she was gone and the young woman at the other end of the phone wouldn't release any information. She would have to wait until tomorrow when she went back to work to find out more information.

***

Ah, her detective work paid off. Karen found out that Sandra had been released earlier that week, leaving with a Toma Kato. Toma Kato, she knew who that was, he owned the building she was living in. She tried to picture him in her head but she didn't recall ever meeting him. But wait, she had. That horrible night of Sandra's assault, he had been talking with the police officers. Karen then remembered seeing him a couple of years ago. Toma and his wife had been regulars at the hospital when his wife was having treatments for her cancer. She remembered, how, towards the end, he wouldn't leave her bedside. He was eventually ordered by the doctor to leave. The doctor had believed that as long as Toma was there, his wife would not let go, that she was hanging on, prolonging her suffering just for a few more moments with him. It had turned out to be true. Less than an hour after being left alone, she had slipped quietly away. Karen had really felt for him. She felt a little better knowing Sandra was in the care of such a good man. She picked up her phone but stopped herself from calling Sandra. Would Sandra even want to talk to her, consider her a friend anymore after not hearing a word from her for months? Maybe one day she would call her, but not today.

***

Sandra looked around her, at the lush green lawn, the fruit trees, the abundant flower garden. It would be such a serene place if it weren't for the Doberman tearing around creating havoc. Sandra feared that he would uproot all of the flowers so she called to him, "Brutus, come!" She thought the name suited him. He was a big, clumsy thing, yet somehow, when standing or sitting still, seemed quite noble. She felt a hand on her shoulder, it was Wanda, "Time for you to head inside, you don't want to over-do it." Sandra nodded in agreement and, with Wanda's help, headed inside.

Once inside her bedroom Sandra collapsed onto the bed. Who would have thought that just sitting could be so strenuous. She took in her surroundings, the large four-poster bed, her chest of drawers and matching vanity. It looked odd without the mirror. It must have gotten broken during the move, or Toma may have had it removed on her account. She had a feeling it was the latter. She would have to ask him about it one day.

***

The moment Sandra entered the hospital she felt like she had never left. It made her feel depressed. "You're quiet today," commented the doctor, "you must be nervous about getting the bandages off." Sandra nodded. "Now don't get too excited about it, and don't expect any miracles," warned the doctor, "it's going to be at least another four weeks until you'll be able to recognize yourself in the mirror, the longer you can hold off taking a peek, the better, that way you're less likely to be disappointed in what you see."

Wanda had taken Sandra to the hospital and was waiting to take her home. Once Sandra emerged, Wanda was careful not to make any comments about her appearance, but kept the conversation light and general.

Toma was back at the house, becoming more agitated as each minute passed. Where were they? The suspense was killing him. He had decided that he wouldn't put off the inevitable any longer, he had to tell her today. He saw the car pull up and hurried to greet them.

Toma was taken aback by Sandra's appearance. But what had he expected? He helped her out of the car and asked if she would mind taking a few moments to speak with him once she felt up to it. She was surprised by the urgency in his voice and suggested that now was as good a time as any. Brutus had come bounding up to greet her and then followed them inside.

Once they were settled in his study Toma cleared his throat. Sandra started to feel fidgety, sensing that something was coming that she wasn't going to like. Toma started, "I apologize for bringing up the assault, but I need for you to realize how I got carried away in the chaos and wasn't thinking clearly." Sandra thought to herself, he's regretting having taken me on, the expense, the... Sandra heard him continue, "Please keep in mind that you were... were no more than a bloody mass. I had no idea who you were then, what you looked like and you were sedated most of the time so the doctors couldn't consult with you..." Sandra was becoming confused, she had no idea where this was going. She pulled Brutus close to her and motioned for Toma to go on. He continued, "When they needed to reconstruct your face, the doctor turned to me for guidance. I made a rash decision. Here, let me show you." He grabbed a photo in a frame that was on the side table next to him and handed it to her. Sandra glanced at the image of a beautiful Asian woman. "She's beautiful." stated Sandra, raising questioning eyes to him. Toma looked into Sandra's eyes, "This is a copy of the photograph that I gave to the doctor. This is the face that I gave you." Silence followed. Sandra was stunned. What was she to say? What did she want to say? How did she feel?

Toma had bowed his head, but found himself raising it now to look at her. He felt compelled to continue, "I didn't realize the magnitude of what I had done, and then, when unpacking your things, I came across photographs of you, and I realized that I had stolen that identity away from you. It also made me think even if you hadn't been famous, what right did I have to take your identity away from you." Sandra tried to speak but couldn't find her voice. Toma said, "Please, don't feel that you need to say anything right now, I can only hope that you won't hate me, and that you might, in time, understand and find it in your heart to forgive me." He got up from his chair, "I'll send Wanda in to help you back to your room."

Wanda walked into the study moments later. As she helped Sandra to her feet she noticed and recognized the photo in Sandra's hand, "I see Mr. Kato has shown you a picture of his late wife. I had the pleasure of knowing her when I was her personal nurse when she was fighting her cancer, both times. She was a beautiful woman, both inside and out. Such a tragedy, the way she suffered through both bouts of her cancer. He was devoted to her to the end. She was his life."

They were almost to Sandra's room when Wanda added, "I though he was never going to snap out of his depression, but I noticed a change for the better in him. Maybe it has to do with your arrival, sometimes the best way to forget your troubles is to take on the troubles of someone else. Well, here we are, will you need help?" Sandra thanked her but said that she thought she could manage on her own.

Sandra walked into the bedroom followed by Brutus. She sat on the edge of her bed and studied the photograph that was still in her hand. She then looked towards the closet. She got up and stiffly and slowly made her way towards it. She scanned the contents of the closet and she caught sight of the cardboard box she was looking for. It was on the floor of the closet, way back in the corner. She got down on her knees, grabbed the box and made her way back to the bed. She sat down and pulled out a handful of photos.

She spread the photos out on the bed. She picked one up. It was her at the age of five. She was making a face, hamming it up for the camera. Another was of her stepping out of a limousine as she arrived at the Academy Awards. She sifted through all of them, each one showing her smiling face. She was so happy back then. How her life had changed. She then picked up the photo of Toma's wife. She was very beautiful. She certainly could have done worse. She looked again at one of her photos. She knew that she was never going to be that person again, no matter what she looked like. Toma had mentioned that she had a famous face. Had she really? Since she had been out of the public eye, she had been able to walk down the street unrecognized. And how many people were knocking on her door with movie deals? Toma had said that he had taken it all away from her, but that wasn't true, it had already been gone long before he ever came into her life. Sandra put the photos back into the cardboard box and then put it back into the closet. She returned to the bed and picked up Toma's wife's picture and placed it on the bedside table. She would return it to him in the morning.

The day had been exhausting both physically and mentally. Sandra didn't feel up to even changing out of her clothes or bothering Wanda to help her. She took off her shoes and slipped under the covers. Brutus, satisfied that his mistress was safe for the night, plopped down on the floor at the end of her bed. Both were asleep within minutes.

Chapter 7

Another clump of weeds were tossed onto the growing pile. Gardening had always been therapeutic for Toma, but today he had already been at it for hours and still there was no reduction in the lines on his furrowed brow. He had finally exhausted himself and now had no choice but to stop and face his thoughts. He sat down on the ground and stuck the garden trowel in the dirt. He had to admit he was worried sick. It was already past noon and Sandra still had not made an appearance. Maybe he would have Wanda check on her. He was about to get up when he felt a gentle hand on his shoulder, and at the same time another hand came into view, holding Mika's framed photograph. "She was a very beautiful woman, tell me about her." Sandra said softly as she sat down beside him on the warm earth.

So there they sat, side by side, as Toma told Sandra about his life with Mika, and his life without her. Toma didn't know if it was because he had been so distraught earlier that he was so filled with emotion but as he spoke he found he couldn't stop the tears from flowing. Sandra listened and almost wept herself at the bittersweet tale, to love someone more than life itself, and for that person to return that love in kind. How often does that happen? Some people never find that kind of happiness, and to have it snatched from you so cruelly. Life was so unfair.

Once Toma's story came to an end, Sandra moved so that she was facing him and took his hands in hers and said, "I feel it an honour to possess such a beautiful face, of a woman that was also beautiful within." Toma who had been looking down, now raised his eyes to Sandra's. She continued, "I don't ever want you to feel guilty for what you did. It's time that I forget the past and look to the future. My new identity is exactly what I need to do that, so if anything, you did me a great service." Toma's response was to draw their clasped hands close to his heart and manage a weak "Thank you."

They disengaged their hands, rose and walked around the yard and Sandra talked about how, as the police had thought it best that her assailant thought her dead, what better opportunity to not be recognizable. She announced that she had been thinking a lot about it and decided that she was also going to change her name. Toma listened and thought it seemed quite drastic, but then again, it also made a lot of sense. He offered, "If you are looking for a surname, you are more than welcome to use mine."

Sandra stopped in her tracks. The thought hadn't crossed her mind, but it would make sense, after all, with her new Asian look, a name like Smith or Jones would be out of place. She thought, Kato, she had recently, out of curiosity, researched the name on the internet, and Kato was actually a form of the name Catherine. She said that she was honoured and would take him up on his generous offer, but if he didn't mind, she was going to use it as her first name. "What will your surname be?" asked Toma. "No surname," replied Sandra, "just Kato, you know, like Madonna, no last name." Toma liked it and nodded his head in approval. Right then and there Sandra decided, goodbye Cassandra Carrington, that young vulnerable woman no longer existed. Say hello to Kato, whoever she may turn out to be. She finally said, "How about some lunch, I don't know about you but I, Kato, am hungry." Her new identity began.

***

It was morning but Kato remained in bed with her eyes closed but then opened them when she felt Brutus licking the palm of her hand, "Okay Brutus, I can take a hint, let's go get something to eat." She got up, grabbed her robe and followed Brutus into the kitchen. That was odd, the kitchen was empty. Usually by this time Mrs. White would be there and whipping up breakfast. She made her way down the hallway to the living room. No one in there either, it was puzzling. She decided to try Toma's study. The door was closed so she gave a quick knock and a questioning "Hello?" Toma replied, "Come in." Kato opened the door and stuck her head in. "Surprise!" Kato jumped in response. So this is where they all were, Toma, Emma, Joan, Brutus, even Wanda was there, although her job of looking after her had been over weeks ago. Toma led her over to a chair and as she sat down everyone gathered around her. He then reached behind his desk and pulled out a flat, rectangular box wrapped up in a bright floral-patterned paper and adorned with a bright yellow ribbon and bow.

"Open it," encouraged Wanda, "and I hope to God you're not one of those people that picks at the paper trying not to rip it!" Kato got the hint and with one swift pull she ripped the paper away and let out a gasp. It was a mirror and she was looking back at a beautiful face. She was breathtaking! She looked to Toma and could only mouth "Thank you." He nodded in acknowledgment and then motioned to Emma who then left but returned moments later with a large birthday cake. Toma announced, "We realize your birthday was months ago on the first of July, but you weren't exactly in any shape to enjoy it then." Wanda, who had been pouring champagne into glasses, passed them around. Toma raised his glass in a toast, "Here's to you Kato!" "To Kato!" the others chorused.

***

The same day that Kato had finally seen her image, all the mirrors were put back in place. Weeks had passed since that day, but she still felt compelled to catch quick glimpses of herself as she passed one. Now, she stopped directly in front of one and studied herself critically. She came to a decision, picked up the phone, made some calls and booked a few appointments. She was thankful that she still had cash that she had on hand before her hospitalization, although she was sure that

Toma wouldn't have hesitated to give her some had she asked.

Toma hadn't questioned her the times when she requested that he drop her off in the downtown area on his way to his office. She had made several trips in the last few weeks but on this particular day he noticed she seemed quite excited when he dropped her off in the morning. It was now afternoon and he arrived at the usual pick up point. He looked around but didn't see her standing there. He was just about to get out of the car when a woman came up to the passenger door. Toma was in shock, it was his Mika! He sat in shock as she opened the door and slid in beside him.

Kato put her hand on Toma's arm and apologized, "I'm so sorry, I wanted to surprise you, I should have realized it would be a shock to you." He blinked and let out a faint, "Kato?" It was Kato, with her hair died a glossy black and contacts that made her eyes a warm brown. The transformation was incredible. The sight of her made his heart sing and break at the same time. It was like the daughter he had always longed for had come into his life at last.

***

That night Kato spent a good part of an hour sitting and studying her new look in the mirror on her vanity. She tried to see herself, but only saw a stranger. A striking woman with cat-like eyes and sleek, glossy hair that fell straight and heavy past her shoulders. It had grown several inches during the time of her recovery. She finally turned and got up from the vanity only to stare straight into a full length mirror. She slowly took each strap of her nightgown and slid them off her shoulders. She lowered her arms and the nightgown fell in one swift movement to the floor. She lowered her gaze which came to rest upon her breasts. They were full and firm. She smiled. The surgeon must have gotten a little carried away on their reconstruction. She cupped them in her hands, feeling their firmness. Using one finger, she gently teased her nipple, and she smiled as it responded to her touch. They seemed to be working just fine. She lowered her eyes further and her hands followed, down past the small of her waist to the curve of her hips, then inwards to the taunt flat surface of her abdomen. She felt a sudden pain, not in her stomach, but in her heart. The heartache of knowing that she may never carry a child. She forced the thought out of her mind as she studied her legs. They looked much as she had remembered them. She went over every inch of her body again, looked closely for scars that were still visible. There were a few, but only noticeable up close. The doctor had recommended a body makeup that would cover them until they disappeared with time.

Kato bent forward to retrieve her nightgown from the floor. As she slid it on, she was aware of every part of her body that it grazed. Yes, it was a very nice body. But what good was it to her? Would she ever let another man close to her? Could she ever trust anyone that much again? She was just about to slide into bed when she remembered her unopened mail. How could she have forgotten? It was the only piece of mail that she had received at this address. She ripped it open and looked at the certificate in her hands. She was now officially Kato.

***

Toma knew the day would come when Kato would decide that she was ready to move out, and he dreaded it. He knew the house was going to seem even emptier than before she had come into his life, so in his mind he had come up with arguments as to why she should stay. He presented them to her now. Where would she go? Where would she work? Also, if she was paying rent, how could she ever expect to raise the money she insisted on repaying him?

Kato bit her bottom lip as she thought about all that he had said, so when Toma suggested a solution, she was more than open to the offer. The secretary at his office was leaving because her husband had been transferred out of town. It would save him the time and trouble of having to interview people. He paid an above-average wage, and if she continued to live in his home, her debt would be paid off that much faster. He went on to say, "Don't think I'm doing you any favours, I have purely selfish reasons. I've come to think of you as a daughter and if you leave now, the emptiness of this house will be unbearable, so I'm asking you to at least think about it."

Kato did think about it. Where *would* she live? How many apartment buildings would allow a big, clumsy Doberman? She wouldn't dream of parting with Brutus. And a job, did she want to go back to being a waitress? Kato had to be realistic, "So when do I start?" Toma beamed. No use starting this week, it's already Thursday, how about Monday?" They shook on it and Toma went into the details of the job. He also added that because she was staying at his home, and his employees knew he doesn't have any children, that it will be best to introduce her as his niece. Kato agreed.

***

She was a mail-order bride, the niece thing was just a cover. She was his niece, but they were having an affair. She wasn't any relation and he took up with her because of her resemblance to his dead wife. And so that's how the rumours went. No one actually approached Kato to confirm or deny any of them, but she caught wind of them. The implications were always there. She saw it in their looks, heard it in their whisperings. She wasn't sure if Toma was also aware of them. If he was, he certainly didn't let on. Of course, whenever he would enter the front office, all whisperings would stop. Staff members who had shunned and ignored her earlier would be friendly towards her, then the minute Toma left the room, all pretense would end. It was a tense situation, but Kato sought solace in her job, working diligently, giving no cause for criticism in that area, or so she thought.

Kato knew something was off the moment she got back from lunch. Tracey, the accounts clerk that relieved Kato for her breaks informed her smugly, "You are to see Mr. Kato in his office immediately." Kato didn't care for the tone of her voice, or the self-satisfied look on her face either. Kato walked tentatively into Toma's office and closed the office door.

Kato had never seen Toma so angry. Actually, she had never seen him angry at all before this moment. He made a motion for her to sit down and she did so quickly without question. Toma started, "The one thing I will not tolerate in this office is offensive behaviour towards my clients!" She was puzzled. Who had she offended? Toma continued, "Mr. Thompson is one of my best clients and I just lost his business today when he refused to renew his lease for his downtown store. He said it was because of the rude service he received when he called in to request the papers be sent to his office as opposed to him coming in to sign them. He said that you outright refused to send them and then told him to come down to the office as it would do him good to get off of his fat ass!" Kato was floored. She didn't remember even talking with a Mr. Thompson. "But I never..." she began, but Toma cut her off short, "Don't deny it, he said that when he asked with whom he was speaking, he was positive that the name given was Kato. There could be no mistake!" Her mind was working fast and she asked, "What day did he say I was speaking with him?" Toma stopped to think, "Last Tuesday, he said it was late afternoon." Kato replied, "Don't you remember? Last Tuesday you had asked me to drop off a deposit at the bank because Elaine was off sick. Tracey was the one answering the phone during that time."

Toma was stunned. Tracey! The thought hadn't even crossed his mind, but of course, it would make sense. Anyone who was capable of such rude behaviour would certainly be capable of such deceit. Toma couldn't apologize enough, "I should never have accused you of such a thing, or believed you capable of such behaviour, please forgive me." Kato accepted his apology and assured him that there were no hard feelings. Toma thought to himself, gracious as ever, now *that* was the Kato he knew. He asked her to run an errand for him, instructing her to leave through the back door. After she left, he tried to decide how he was going to handle the situation.

***

Well that was that! She had finally found a way to get rid of her. Tracey had dislike Kato the minute she had set eyes on her. The combination of drop dead gorgeous and a killer body was more competition than even Tracey could handle. She saw the way the men looked at Kato when they stopped in to the office. Well with little Ms. Perfect gone she would again be the one getting all of the looks. Lost in her thoughts, Tracey jumped when Elaine said, "Tracey, I'm supposed to answer the phone for you, Mr. Kato wants a word with you, *now*!"

***

Toma's eyes had certainly been opened. When he confronted Tracey, he had not expected the vicious reaction he received. She was like a mad dog and he almost expected her to start foaming at the mouth. The ugly truth came out. Not only her confession, but also about the rumours circulating about Kato and Toma's relationship. He was left with no doubt in his mind about dismissing Tracey. Never before had he come across such a venomous person, He was glad to be rid of this poison.

After Tracey had stormed out, Toma found himself faced with a new dilemma. He had had his suspicions about rumours going around, but he didn't realize the extent of them, or the brunt of it that Kato had received. He was going to see that things changed around here, although he suspected that the main perpetrator had just left his office.

He looked at the calendar on his desk. Christmas was fast approaching. Aside from the annual Christmas office party, he had gotten out of the habit of celebrating the season. This year he was going to have a Christmas tree in his home. And not just a tree, a tall touching the ceiling tree, decorated to the hilt. Christmas was going to return to the Kato home!

Chapter 8

"Sandra?" Karen asked quizzically. The voice *sounded* like Sandra's but the woman standing at her apartment door was *not* Sandra. Karen shook her head in disbelief. Kato explained, "Actually, technically I'm not Sandra Carrington anymore, I've legally changed my name to Kato." Karen was still not convinced so Kato continued, "Okay, here's something only Sandra Carrington would know about you, remember that sweltering hot night when we mixed up that big batch of margaritas, and got totally plastered up on the rooftop patio. You decided to do a little strip-ease for the neighbours, that is, until you realized there were actually neighbours that were watching." Karen was flabbergasted, "Oh my God! How could I forget? That one guy wouldn't leave me alone for months after that! I never told a soul about that night!"

The truth hit Karen and she began to cry, "So many times I wanted to call you, but chickened out. I can't believe you're even talking to me. Come," Karen motioned Kato inside, "tell me what happened, I want to hear it all." Hours passed as Kato told Karen all that had happened to her. Karen in turn told Kato about her extended trip and what had been going on at work, "Speaking of work, Barbara, one of the nurses, has pulled some strings to get a group of us invited to a big Christmas bash, you've got to come!" Karen saw Kato hesitate and added, "We've been to a few of these parties put on by some of the doctors before. It's usually the same old crowds, but once in a while they invite celebrities that the doctors get to know after they've treated them. Please, say you'll come, it will be fun!" Fun, Kato thought, when was the last time she could honestly say she went out and had some fun. She agreed to go. Karen gave her a quick hug and said before Kato could change her mind, "It's settled then, I'll see you Saturday!"

***

Saturday evening Kato found herself feeling nervous. This would be her first social outing as Kato. She had met people through work of course, but you couldn't really count them, that was just business. At the party people would be asking her questions about herself, personal questions about where she grew up, her family and any number of things. She had to compose herself, she could pull this off, after all, she was an actor wasn't she?

Kato pulled on a slim-fitting pair of black pants and a simple camisole top covered in black sequins. A pair of emerald drop earrings that had belonged to her mother added a touch of festive colour. She took one last look in the mirror, trying to feel some connection to the reflection that stared back at her. It was just a role she told herself, the role of Kato.

***

Kato thanked Toma for the ride and assured him that she would call a taxi when she was ready to leave. The outside of the house was adorned with blinking Christmas lights and she could see a tree in the window, glittering with ornaments and lights. When she got to the front door she decided to just let herself in, nobody was going to hear the doorbell over the blaring music.

Kato looked around the room and spotted Karen in a far corner talking and laughing with a group of women. Karen spotted her and waved her over. Kato stepped forward but stopped when a hand on her arm detained her. She looked up to see an attractive man with dark hair, and a beard and mustache. The beard was short and neatly trimmed and somehow gave him a devilish air. He was looking down at her and she could see in his eyes that he liked what he saw. He was about to say something but was stopped short by Karen's "Down boy, don't make me get out the fire hose!" Karen grabbed Kato's free arm and dragged her away, "Run, don't walk away from that one, he's bad news." "Who is he?" Kato asked. "Craig Paul," answered Karen, then she pointed towards a fireplace off to the side, "and you see the uh, pleasantly plump brunette over there?" Kato nodded. Karen continued, "That's his forever forgiving girlfriend."

Karen brought them to a halt in front of the group she had been talking to earlier. Vera was the first one to speak, "So you already had to be rescued from 'the boyfriend' I see." Barbara added, "We call him that because he has forever been Julie's boyfriend, yet wanting to be 'the boyfriend' of everyone else at the same time." Kato was confused, "But if he's interest in other women, why doesn't he just break it off with her?" Jen piped in, "We all have our theories." Vera gave her theory, "I think it's like this, he most likely found her attractive when they first met, but her appearance changed over the years, but he would feel guilty breaking it off," then Vera continued in a whisper, "after all, he was her *first*." Barbara argued, "I think he's too damn chicken to take a chance and seriously go after someone he does want and second, it's the money, I mean, even though they aren't married, he somehow wangled his way into her mommy and daddy's mansion. He's not going to give that up, he's got it made." Kato found it hard to understand how anyone could stay with someone that they didn't wholeheartedly want to be with.

"Hey, enough of that everyone, it's party time!" said Karen and continued with introductions, "Kato, this is Vera, Barbara and Jen, everyone, this is Kato." Kato injected, "Actually I've met all of you at one point in time, but you would have known me as Sandra Carrington. I was a patient at the hospital for quite some time. All three women were shocked. "You're *her*,", exclaimed Barbara, "wow! The doctors did an excellent job!" Vera added, "Ya, all the guys in this room are drooling over you, even Mike. Maybe you can distract him and get him off of Barbara's back." Karen interjected, "Come on, give her a break, I wouldn't wish Mike upon my worst enemy." Kato's curiosity was peaked, "What's wrong with him?" Barbara explained, "Married. He propositioned me and I told him in no uncertain terms that I had no use for married men, that I'm a *whole* woman, and as a *whole* woman I need a *whole* man, not half of one or whatever portion he would decide to offer me. And besides that, call me a selfish person but I don't like to share!" "I have to agree with you there," said Vera, "it would be like grabbing an ice cream cone that a woman had just finished licking all over and then licking it yourself, ugh! And no matter how much I might like that flavour, I'd decline and then go out and get my own ice cream cone thank you very much. And who knows, I may even find a flavour I like even better!" Kato had to smile at their banter. Seeing Kato's smile, Karen said, "That's better. It's time to get into the spirit of Christmas, or at least some Christmas spirits, let's get you a drink."

"Bartender, get us some drinks and quick!" Karen said as her and Kato came up to the make-shift bar. The man behind the bar had his back towards them but at the sound of Karen's voice turned around. That's when Kato was hit with the full force of his charm. Jet black curly hair fell over his forehead, almost falling into his warm, brown eyes, and when he smiled, she smiled back. Karen didn't miss the exchange of looks and was quick to make introductions, "Kato, this is Rudy, Rudy, Kato." She then made a lame excuse about having to get back to the other woman and left the two alone.

"Where's Kato?" asked Barbara, "I hope you didn't leave her to the wolves." Karen replied, "No, I left her in the hands of Rudy, I can't say I know him that well but he seems like an okay guy." "Geez," said Vera, "she's here for what, maybe a hour, and she's already hooked someone." She added jokingly, "From now on when you bring a friend along, make sure she's ugly, okay?"

Kato stayed and talked with Rudy for about twenty minutes, during which time Rudy manged to get her phone number and address, and a firmed up date for the following weekend. Kato excused herself and set off on a quest to find the washroom. She managed to get as far as the hallway before her path was blocked by an imposing figure. She tried to slip by him, but a muscular arm stopped her. "Take a hint Ray, the lady doesn't want your attention." said a voice, low, but with authority. Ray withdrew his arm and took his leave. Kato smiled gratefully at her rescuer, a well dressed older man with short, spiked gray hair. He offered his arm, "Allow me to escort you to your destination, I'll take a wild guess that it's the powder room?" Kato nodded and took his arm. He led her to a door at the end of the hallway, then took his leave.

After Kato left the quiet of the bathroom she found the loud music quite jarring in contrast, and the party seemed to get rowdier with each passing minute. Her head began to ache and she went in search of Karen and her hostess to say her goodbyes.

***

It felt so good to be home. Brutus greeted Kato and followed her to her bedroom. As usual he waited for his mistress to settle into bed before he took his place on the floor at the end of the bed. Kato couldn't sleep. Thoughts of Rudy kept going through her mind. How much should she tell him about herself? Could she trust him with the truth, her true identity? She shuddered to think what the tabloids would do with the information if they ever got a hold of it. But then again, if she didn't tell him, and he found out later, he was sure to feel betrayed. She thought back to how she had felt when she had deliberately been betrayed by Zack, or whoever the hell he really was. She gave herself a mental shake. For God's sake, she was going on one date with the guy. She might decide she didn't want to see him again after that, or he might never call her again. She would just have to wait and see where it went before she made any decision. She closed her eyes, black curly hair, warm brown eyes and a charming smile were the last images she saw in her mind before drifting off to sleep.

***

In the hospital staff room Barbara said to Karen, "Okay, remember how at the party Vera was kidding about next time you brought a friend along to make sure she was ugly?" Karen nodded. Barbara continued, "Well I'm going to say the same thing, but *I'm* not kidding. After she left she was all that the men were talking about, even John Macy." "John Macy!" Karen exclaimed, "Wow! She really did make an impression!" Barbara said, "Speaking of next time, don't make any plans for New Year's Eve, I'm working on one of the doctors to get an invite for all of us but nothing is firmed up yet. I'll keep you posted." Karen was intrigued as she watched Barbara walk out of the room. There was never a dull moment when Barbara was around.

***

Kato's hands were shaking so much that she could barely put her makeup on. Maybe she just wasn't ready for this yet. But it was too late to back out now, Rudy was due to pick her up at any moment. He had promised her dinner, cooked by a world-class chef, himself. Actually he wasn't a chef, cooking was simply a hobby of his and he had told her that he wanted to show off his culinary skills. She felt extremely nervous about the fact that the date was going to be at his place. What if the conversation fell flat? The silence would be so awkward. She took a little comfort in knowing that they wouldn't be going very far. When she talked with Rudy at the party she discovered that he also lived in the Santa Monica area quite close to Toma's house. If worse came to worse, she could always grab a taxi home. She didn't have any more time to think about it. Brutus started barking, announcing Rudy's arrival.

Kato went to greet Rudy but Toma had beat her to it. The two men had already introduced themselves by the time she made her way to the front door. Rudy turned towards her and looked appreciatively at her in the sleek black leggings that clung to her shapely legs and the long black sweater that skimmed her slim hips. Rudy thought she looked like a sleek black cat. She greeted him with a smile and said goodbye to Toma. She thought fondly of how protective Toma was and it warmed her heart. She had always felt that she had missed out by not having a father growing up.

It took less than ten minutes to get to Rudy's place. Kato found her stomach was still in knots as the late model corvette came to a stop. She wasn't very knowledgeable about cars, but she guessed it to be from the '70s. It was in good shape though so it must have been restored at some point. Rudy swiftly got out of the car and came to open her door, then they were on their way inside.

Moments after they were inside, Rudy went to an already uncorked bottle of red wine and poured some into a couple of wine glasses. Kato wasn't totally comfortable with his swiftness, he seemed just a little too smooth and practiced for her liking. He led her into the living room and told her to make herself comfortable while he prepared their meal. After Rudy went into the kitchen, she looked around the room. The decor was southwest and had a casual, comfortable look about it. She wondered whose taste it was as Rudy had told her that he shared the house with two other bachelors. They had apparently made themselves scarce tonight. She turned her attention to the large double doors facing the beach. The sun had set a while ago and the water looked dark and murky. She looked up to the sky and at the twinkling stars, becoming mesmerized.

Kato wasn't sure how long she had been standing there, or what made her turn around, but when she did, she was shocked. Rudy was there, in the doorway, staring at her. The zipper of his pants was down, and he had his penis in his hand and was jerking off. Her wine glass slipped out of her hand and the crash as it hit the hardwood floor stopped Rudy short. She ran past him through the doorway and slowed down only to grab her shoes and purse. She hadn't thought to bring her cell phone with her, so when she ran out the front door, she stopped at a house a couple of doors down that had its lights on. Only then did she take the time to put her shoes on.

A man in his mid-thirties answered the door, closely followed by a woman about the same age. It looked like they had been sharing a romantic dinner, and under normal circumstances Kato wouldn't have thought of intruding, but these were not normal circumstances. Not by a long shot! Kato made up a lame story about how she was in the car with her boyfriend, they had fought and she got out of the car, and now needed to get home. The woman in the house called a taxi for her and then invited her inside to wait for it to come.

Thankfully the taxi was there within minutes and Kato was on her way home. Home. She never wanted to leave its protective walls again. She just wanted to hide away from the world, she didn't want to have to face reality or deal with people again for as long as she lived! She paid the driver and ran to the front door.

Toma was in his study when he heard Kato come in. It seemed not that long ago that she had left. He looked up at the clock, no, she hadn't been gone that long at all. He was about to get up to greet her, but stayed put when he heard her run past the study door and down the hallway to her room. No. Best to leave any talking until morning, maybe not even then if she didn't bring up the subject. The subject did come up, but not with Toma. As soon as Kato got to her bedroom she called Karen.

***

Karen was dumfounded, "He what? I can't believe it! Not Rudy!" Kato replied, "I can hardly believe it myself, it was like a bad dream." Karen apologized, "I'm so sorry, I would never have introduced you to him had I known what a pervert he is. But who would have guessed, he seemed so, *normal*! I hope you reported it to the police." "I didn't think of it at the time." replied Kato, "I suppose I should have though, I'd hate to think that some other unsuspecting woman might have to go through the same thing." "Also," stressed Karen, "it would have sent a message to the jerk, loud and clear, that such dirty deeds are totally unacceptable, *and illegal*!"

A thought hit Karen, "Oh my God! I see Rudy every day at work, I won't be able to look him in the eyes again! Why did you have to tell me this?" Kato was unsympathetic, "Imagine how I feel! Whatever you do, don't invite me to another function if he's going to be there." "You've got yourself a deal." Karen agreed.

***

After Karen hung up with Kato she couldn't help herself, she called Barbara. She hoped that Kato didn't feel that she was breaking a confidence, but after all, she did feel obligated to tell her fellow co-workers there was a pervert in their midst. And okay, thought Karen, this was just too bizarre and dishy a story to keep to herself.

***

The next morning all through breakfast Kato still hadn't mentioned her evening out to Toma and he resigned himself to never knowing what had transpired that night. He studied her face as she ate her breakfast. She was still quieter than usual but otherwise seemed none the worse for wear. He had an idea that he thought might draw her out. He cleared his throat before saying, "There's something that I would like your assistance with today." Kato was puzzled, it was the weekend and she had the day off. It wasn't like Toma to make her work on the weekends. Toma saw her expression and said, "Don't look so serious, I just wanted you to help me pick out a Christmas tree. Mika always accused me of bringing home the most pathetic-looking tree on the lot, so unless you want a Charlie Brown tree, it would be in your best interest to come with me." Kato smiled, "In that case, just try to stop me from coming along." She excused herself from the table to get ready and almost skipped to her room.

Chapter 9

Twinkling lights shone brightly, casting a warm glow on delicate glass baubles, reflecting rainbows of light onto silver garland. Snowflakes glittered, stars sparkled and jolly Santa Claus' winked at golden angels. Toma looked upon the grand tree and Christmas' past came to mind. He remembered how, throughout the years, Mika had come to collect this treasure trove of ornaments. All of them had been lovingly hand-picked by her, making each and every one something special. Tears welled up in his eyes. He had deprived himself of these precious memories the last few years.

Kato was lost in her own thoughts. The sight brought her back to her childhood when Christmas was a magical time. She had been so innocent, so happy. But then memories of last Christmas and the time following it clouded her mind. Thoughts of Zack, her unborn baby, the baby she could have been holding in her arms right now had things turned out differently.

The silence was stretching between them, broken suddenly by the arrival of Brutus. His reaction to the sight of the giant tree was comical. He crouched down, letting out low growls, alternating with little high-pitched yelps. He finally got up enough courage to crawl over on his belly and put his nose to the base of the trunk. "No! Brutus! Stop!" Kato could barely get the words out for laughing. She had anticipated his intentions just in time and pulled him away from the tree just as Brutus was raising his leg. She led him to the back door and ushered him outside.

After Kato had returned from putting Brutus outside, Toma mentioned the staff Christmas party to her. It was going to be held at the office that coming Friday, starting right after closing time. She gave a weak smile and said she was looking forward to it. She then excused herself, saying that she was going to make an early night of it.

Once inside her bedroom Kato collapsed onto her bed. The staff Christmas party. How she dreaded the thought of it. Toma had thought that with the departure of Tracey all of the problems and tensions had disappeared but nothing could have been further from the truth. There were those staff members that were still influenced by Tracey and they had set out to make her life miserable. She hadn't been able to bring herself to tell Toma the truth, what could he do, fire them all? So instead she remained quiet, taking their abuse, swallowing her pride. With each day she was finding it harder and harder to get up and face the day. She wasn't sure how much longer she could take the abuse.

***

"Kato!" Kato heard her name being called yet again. This time it was coming from right outside her door and was accompanied by a loud knock. Toma sounded quite alarmed and Kato felt obliged to respond, "I'm sorry, I don't feel well today, I'm afraid I won't be able to go in to work." Toma was disappointed, "But it's Friday, the staff Christmas party is tonight." She was disappointed in herself when she replied, "I know, I'm really sorry." She felt even worse when Toma said a quiet "Okay." before she heard him walk away down the hallway.

Kato felt bad about deceiving Toma but she just couldn't face an entire evening in the company of those back-stabbing bitches. She could feel herself becoming angry, not at them, but at herself. She shouldn't have let them get to her, she was made of sterner stuff than that.

As the day dragged on Kato's anger turned to boredom and she grabbed her phone on the first ring, "Hello?" It was Karen inviting her to a New Year's Eve bash that Barbara had managed to wangle some invitations to. One of the doctors at the hospital, who Barbara knew quite well, had treated a celebrity who had extended an invitation to the doctor and any number of guests that he wanted to bring. Karen explained, "It's going to be a masquerade ball and everyone is supposed to dress up as a well known character, present or past, real or fictional." Kato didn't even hesitate before accepting, she was ready for some fun.

After she hung up Kato turned her attention to what costume she could wear. She would have a lot to choose from. At one time her mother had been on quite friendly terms with a woman in wardrobe at one of the studios. Many times her mother had been able to take home ensembles that caught her eye. She hunted through the massive closet to see what she could find.

***

"How are you feeling today?" inquired Toma. Kato felt a twinge of guilt when she replied, "Much better thanks, it must have been a 24-hour bug." "Well here's something that should make you feel better, your Christmas bonus." said Toma as he held out an envelope to her. She took the envelope and removed the cheque, then opened her mouth ready to protest, but Toma spoke first, "No, it's not too much, everyone gets the same amount and believe me, you've earned it." She smiled and graciously thanked him, then started to eat her breakfast. She hadn't eaten much the day before and now she was ravenous.

***

It was Christmas day! Kato looked at the clock, eight o'clock, perfect. She could put Toma's gift under the tree undetected. She crept down the hallway, trying to be as quiet as possible. She slipped into the living room and crouched down beside the tree. She almost dropped the present when she heard "Merry Christmas!" Toma must have had the same idea because there he was, gift in hand. He extended the wrapped package to her and she responded in kind, "Merry Christmas!" They both sat on the floor opening their respective gifts.

Toma had managed to unwrap his first. Tears came to his eyes as he held the portrait in front of him. It was his favourite picture of Mika, but not the tiny faded cracked picture he had looked at the last few years. This was a large reproduction done in vivid colours, painted in oils by a skilled artist. His voice cracked as he thanked her.

Kato could tell he liked the gift and was pleased. She had racked her brain trying to figure out what to get a man who had everything, everything but what he really wanted, his Mika. She couldn't bring her back, so this was the next best thing.

Kato could feel Toma's eyes on her as she finally tore off the wrapping paper from her gift and lifted the lid. Her breath was taken away at what she saw nestled in the velvet lining of the box. In a white gold setting, five marquis-shaped diamonds formed a perfect star. It hung from a delicate white gold chain. She was speechless. Toma took the necklace from the box and fastened the chain around her neck as he said, "I remembered the story that you had told me, the one about your mother and what she had said to you, *star light, star bright, first star I see tonight, I wish I may, I wish I might be that star I see tonight.* You need to keep sight of that star Cassandra." Cassandra. She had lost sight of who she was, where she was going. She was existing, but not living, and certainly not living her dream. But what was her dream? She had even lost sight of that. Toma put a hand on her shoulder and broke the silence, "Let's have some breakfast. Mrs. White has the day off so you'll have to settle for my cooking. I hope you like pancakes because that's the extent of my culinary skills."

Once in the kitchen she could hear scratching and whining at the outside door. She opened it and in bounded Brutus. She went to her bedroom and brought him back a large rawhide bone. "Well that should keep him busy for the rest of the day." commented Toma. Breakfast was made and they sat down to enjoy it, each lost in their own thoughts. Kato had visions dancing in her head, but they weren't of sugar plums, they were of her, marching to the beat of twelve drummers drumming, when all she wanted to do was dance, dance to the beat of a different drum, her own.

***

Where was that mask? Kato knew it was around somewhere, and it was driving her nuts that she couldn't find it, one couldn't go to a masked ball without a mask. Finally! It was in the last box of course. She put it on carefully so as not to smudge her elaborate eye makeup. She adjusted the snake bracelet on her upper arm and took one last look in the mirror. Cleopatra lives! She was beginning to have her doubts about the costume which was designed to show quite a bit of skin. The doorbell rang. Karen had offered to pick her up and that would be her now. There wasn't any time for her to change her mind, or her costume.

***

It was an odd mix. Kato watched Mark Twain walk past with Queen Victoria, Shakespeare talking with Napoleon and W.C. Fields. She was so busy people watching that she didn't notice that she herself was being watched.

Viktor hadn't been sure about coming to the party. He had completed a real estate deal for the celebrity who was putting it on and had been insistant that he come. Viktor thought that it could be a good opportunity to make some connections, so he came, but alone. He was considering it a business obligation more than a social occasion as he move among the crowd.

Then he spotted her. Viktor couldn't take his eyes off of her, she was stunning and walked with such grace, and yet, she seemed totally unaware of her beauty and the effect it was having on every man in the room. Who was she? He felt an over-whelming urge to lift her mask and see her beauty in its entirety. His body seemed to move on its own accord towards her.

***

"I was never so insulted in my life!" Vera said vehemently. Karen asked, "Tony asked you to move in with him, how could you take that as an insult?" Vera replied, "Living together, what the hell is that? If he wants someone to help pay the bills he can get himself a roommate. Now, if he wants to talk commitment, then maybe I'll listen." Jen piped in, "But you said he mentioned maybe having a child together, that's a big commitment." Vera became more livid, "Oh ya, he even said that the kid could have his last name, well what about me? I'm the one who would ruin my figure, waddle around like a duck for nine months, never mind giving up drinking for that time. Oh ya, then there's hemorrhoids, varicose veins and stretch marks, and of course probably a good full day of hard labour, but am *I worthy* of his name? Apparently not!" Jen said laughingly, "Okay, you win!"

When Vera had gone on her rant about the drawbacks of pregnancy she had made elaborate gestures including waddling around like a duck, which Kato found quite comical and she was laughing so hard that it brought tears to her eyes. She turned away from the group and removed her mask in order to wipe them away.

Kato had just brushed her finger across her eye when she saw him. His features were strong, and behind the Zorro mask were piercing blue eyes, fringed with long dark lashes. He removed his black hat with a flourish as he bowed before her, exposing his thick, dark brown hair that was slicked back from his forehead. Once he straightened he flashed her a brilliant white smile. A smile that the original Zorro would have envied. Above that smile was a thin mustache drawn on with a black eyebrow pencil. Because Viktor had received the invitation so late, there hadn't been enough time to grow a real one.

He introduced himself as Viktor Cross, then was stunned into silence. She was breathtaking, but something was a little off. Her eyes. Because she looked to be of Asian descent he had expected to see brown eyes, but staring back at him was one brown eye and one green eye. But of course, contacts. She had just rubbed her eyes and she must have lost one.

Kato couldn't quite figure him out. He tells her his name, then does nothing but stare, and now, without a word, he was taking her hands in his. She broke the silence, "Kato." He looked up at her briefly then back down at her hands. She felt a light touch on her index finger and then focused on his hand as he held it up to her face. "I believe you lost this." he explained. She noticed that he was holding out one of her contacts. She thanked him and then excused herself to go put it back in.

Viktor watched her go. When he was looking for the wayward contact he had expected to find a green one, but instead it turned out to be brown. Why, he wondered, would someone with such amazing green eyes hide them? He was intrigued by this Kato. He guessed that she might be just part Asian, what with her green eyes and her above average height. But where did she come from? Why had he never come across this beauty before? And how could he get to know her better? Damn! His cell phone was ringing. Who would be calling him on New Year's Eve?

***

Kato came back from the washroom, half-hoping to catch a glimpse of Viktor, but didn't see him anywhere. She caught sight of Karen's long dark curls and Jen's ash blonde hair and headed in that direction. She thought of how well their costumes suited them. Karen's Catwoman outfit suited her slim athletic build and Jen made a perfect Tinkerbell with her petite pixie looks. On the other hand she had almost not recognized Barbara, her brown wavy hair covered by the platinum blonde wig. Kato had to admit though that the Mae West costume suited both her buxom figure and her personality to a tee. Then there was Vera. It didn't surprise Kato that she had come as Zsa Zsa Gabor, she bore a resemblance to her and Vera was one for glitz and glam. Barbara and Vera were exchanging strong viewpoints on yet another subject but the conversation switched to Kato as she joined the group. Barbara asked, "How do you do it?" Yes chimed in Vera, "How do you find these to die for men. Next time we'll have to dress you up in a burlap sack to give the rest of us a fighting chance." Barbara said to Vera, "Hey, what are you griping about, you've got your man, well, sort of." Karen quickly cut in, "Let's not get on the subject of Tony again, come on girls, happy thoughts! Cheers!"

They all raised their glasses and said in unison, "Cheers!"

***

The night wore on and as much as Kato was enjoying the company and the music, she found her thoughts returning to last New Year's Eve in New York with Zack. Just when she thought that she had forgotten about him, there he was, back to haunt her. It was nearing midnight and she couldn't face seeing all of the happy couples bringing in the new year with their passionate kisses. She headed out into the night air. It was quite cool and she began to shiver, yet she refused to go back inside until after the count down was over. She closed here eyes as the countdown started, her mind focused on Zack and the special kiss they had shared to celebrate the new year the year before. But as the countdown continued her vision changed and instead of being in an embrace with Zack she imagined herself in the arms of a man with dark brown hair, his hair free of the hat that had been covering it, and strands falling over his forehead, almost hiding one of his piercing blue eyes. She was no longer aware of the cool air around her as the image of Viktor became clearer in her mind.

***

It wasn't fair, Viktor thought. Why did she have to pick tonight of all nights to go into labour? His annoyance turned to worry. Susan had been in hard labour now for several hours. To him it seemed like days. He looked down at her, her face and hair drenched in sweat. She looked totally exhausted. To her this must seem like it has been going on for an eternity. He glanced at the doctor, his brow furrowed. Another doctor had been summoned and he now came through the door. They took a few moments to consult, then the room was a flurry of activity as they prepared the patient for a C-section.

Viktor was in the waiting room when the nurse came out to announce, "It's a girl!" A girl thought Viktor, his earlier annoyance was gone and replaced with joy. Joy and an overwhelming sense of pride. He rushed into Susan's room and went to her side. He looked at her face with love. He felt love for this woman and the child she had just bore. He bent down to give her a kiss on the forehead.

"Would you like to hold her?" asked the nurse. Viktor looked at the nurse holding out the red-faced bundle to him. His voice cracked as he spoke, "Yes please." He held out his arms. The small warm body was feather-light in his arms and he whispered, "Well hello there young lady. You don't know me yet, but you will. And you're going to like me, yes you will, because I'm going to spoil you rotten, yes I am, because that's what uncles do."

He felt exhausted and he wasn't even the one who had been in labour for hours. He remembered the annoyance he felt when his sister Susan had told him that her husband Rod was going to be out of the country on business from December through to April. He had felt put upon when asked if he could step in when Susan went into labour while Rod was away. Now he felt pity, pity for Rod for having to miss this moment. It was lost to him forever. Rod's loss, but his gain Viktor thought as he gazed lovingly down at his niece.

Chapter 10

They wanted her? Kato didn't understand. How would they even know about her? She was full of questions. "Have you heard of a Mr. John Macy?" asked the voice on the other end of the phone. Kato was drawing a blank. The voice continued, "He had found talent for us in the past and was quite impressed with you when he spotted you at a Christmas party. He did manage to get a few candid shots of you at the party, and we like what we've seen but want the opportunity to see you in person and get some professional shots and go from there. We would have reached you earlier but it took us awhile to track you down." Kato's head was spinning. She thought back to the night of the Christmas party. Of course, the distinguished gentleman who had come to her rescue. He had been taking a few shots with his cell phone but so were a lot of the other guests so she hadn't really thought anything about it. Kato tried to concentrate on the instructions the person on the other end of the phone was giving her.

A model, Kato thought as the phone call ended. Was that what she was destined to be? She would find out next Tuesday. She wanted to leave for New York a couple of days before that just to get her bearings a bit before she had to be at the agency. She would have to talk with Toma about taking the time off of work. Her hand went to the diamond star that hung around her neck.   She had a feeling that he would insist on her going.

As Kato had suspected he would be, Toma was thrilled. In fact, the day he dropped her off at the airport he seemed to be even more nervous than she was.   Once airborne, she sat back and began to think of the possibilities.   The financial freedom.   She could pay Toma off in one lump sum.   She new the money was a non-issue with him, he certainly didn't need the money and was in no hurry to get it back, but to her it was always there, a debt owed.   She had to pay it back if only to appease herself.

As the plane came in for a landing Kato remembered the time she had seen the same scene with Zack.   She began to get angry with herself.   Just when she thought she had been able to get him out of her mind once and for all, there he was again.   She became determined. She was going to finally get him out her mind and make a new life for herself.

***

"Amazing!" said one.   "She has the face of today," said another, continuing, "she'll appeal to our growing Asian market, and our American clients as well."   "She's a hot commodity, money in the bank!" piped in another. Kato tried not to let all the excitement and hype carry her away.   Toma had given her the name and number of a reputable lawyer should it turn out that they wanted her to sign anything. So at the end of the day she had to tell them that she would get back to them.

The next week was a blur and Kato's head was still spinning after the contract was signed. And with the exorbitant amount of money she was going to end up with she was going to be able to pay Toma in full and then some. And this was just the beginning. She called Toma to tell him the good news.

***

After Toma hung up the phone from talking with Kato he slumped into a chair. He was happy for her, but she would be moving on, leaving his home and his life. Both would seem very empty. Brutus must have sensed his sadness, he padded into the room and rested his head on Toma's lap. Toma absently stroked the dog's head and Brutus started to whine. Toma looked down at Brutus and said, "You miss her too, don't you boy?"

***

Karen couldn't have been happier for Kato. "That's great! We'll have to celebrate! Hey, your birthday is next week, we'll celebrate then. Hmm, twenty-one years old, aren't you a little old to be a model? After all, you're not fifteen anymore." Karen teased.

***

"Happy Birthday!" they chorused. Kato felt embarrassed as Karen, Jen and Barbara made a fuss and placed a birthday cake with twenty-one candles on it in front of her. "Make a wish!" said Jen. Kato stopped to think. Her present circumstances were like a wish come true already, she was going next week to Europe to model on runways, then on her return to the United States was going to have her face on the cover of one of the top fashion magazines. What more could she ask for? What more did she want? The image of a dashing figure came into her mind. A man behind a Zorro mask. "Oh blow the damn things out before they call the fire department," complained Barbara, "Christ, it's getting hot in here!" Karen said to Barbara, "Well if you find it hot now, just wait until you see what just walked through the door!" They all turned to the front of the pub and watched as a group of half a dozen handsome young men walked through the door. But then the women turned their attention to the woman walking in behind them.

"Vera!" Barbara called out and continued once Vera was at their table, "Where have you been? We were about to send out a search party! Speaking of parties, let's get moving on this one, blow!" Barbara ordered Kato. Kato quickly complied and they all cheered as she blew out every one. "Well I don't know what you wished for, but I know my wish came true, check it out." said Vera as she extended her left hand and wiggled her ring finger which held a large flashy solitaire diamond. "Oh my God!" exclaimed Barbara, "How did you finally get Tony to commit?"

Vera sat herself down before commenting. "Well I told him right out that there was no way I was going through the pain and trouble of having his kids if he didn't think that I was worthy of his name. He started to give me this cock and bull excuse that men can't be expected to know what women want if women don't even know themselves. Well I told *him*! I told him that I know *exactly* what women want. We want to feel *special* and that he wasn't exactly filling the bill, and that if he couldn't make me feel special, that I might as well go out right now and find someone that would!" Vera glanced around and yelled out to no one in particular, "Hear that guys? Take note! That's *all* a woman wants from a man! All she wants is for him to make her feel *special*!" Vera turned back towards the table, "Now every man in this bar would know the answer to that age old question, but they don't and you know why? Because being typical men, they weren't *listening*!" She waved her hand in the air as if to dismiss them all.

Barbara piped in "Getting back to you and Tony, what did he say?" Vera replied, "Nothing. I started to walk out when he grabbed me by the arm and dragged me down the street until we got to a jewelry store. We went inside and he bought me this right then and there." Karen concluded, "Ah that's why you were so late getting here." Vera retorted, "Heck no, it took me just minutes to pick out the ring, but then we went back and uh, celebrated our engagement." Karen smiled and raised her glass, "To celebrations!"

***

Some looked at Kato in disdain, others didn't even look her way, so engrossed were they in their own images staring back at them in the mirrors. Then there were the ones that looked down their noses at her, literally. Kato at five-ten had never thought of herself as short, but standing amongst these models, she felt not only of small stature but also inferior somehow. Maybe it was because she felt like a farce, after all, she wasn't a model, she had no training. She studied the other women, their posture, their walks. The best way for her to feel like a model was to pretend she was playing the role of one. She could do this.

In this particular fashion show Kato was to model just one outfit. It was the highlight of the clothing line being shown and many of the other models were resentful that this newcomer was going to receive this special honour. The peacock blue halter-necked evening gown was floor length with a high slit on one side. The raw silk was fluid, yet stiff enough to support the thousands of multi-coloured crystal beads that formed a sideways facing peacock head and the embroidered neck of the bird on the bodice. The peacock wrapped around to the low-cut back, the embroidered tail sweeping down the back to the hem of the dress.

The designer came over to ensure his masterpiece was being properly displayed. The model's hair had been put up on top of her head, piled high and in large loops. The makeup was dramatic and flawless. He approved the heavy gold earrings that hung almost to her shoulders, but what was that around her neck? It was detracting from the peacock head. It would have to go. He motioned to one of his assistants and ordered her to remove the necklace. The assistant approached Kato, "The necklace has to go." Kato put her hand on the star hanging from the chain. She had put it on that morning, and once she was helped into the dress she had automatically adjusted the star so that it sat over top of the dress. She fumbled with the clasp and was finally able to undo it. The assistant became impatient, "Come on! You're on now!" Kato had no choice but to leave the necklace on the table she was standing in front of. She then held her head high and walked onto the runway.

The crowd had been impressed throughout the entire show, but once they caught sight of Kato in the stunning dress, everyone in the room was on their feet. They were all still standing when the designer made his appearance to close the show.

Once backstage, Kato made a bee-line to the table where she had left her necklace, but it was gone. An assistant came to help her out of the dress but she brushed her away. She had to get the necklace back, it was part of her!

Kato looked frantically through the few objects on the table, then down on the floor, nothing! She made her way through the room, looking at each model to see if any of them was wearing it. Then she noticed two models talking and laughing at the doorway. Kato barely noticed the model who had her back to her, her eyes were focused on the one with blonde curls cascading down onto her shoulders. The one with Kato's diamond star around her neck. Kato couldn't speak, she was so furious. Purposefully, she walked up to the blonde, grabbed the star and with one quick pull, yanked so hard that the chain snapped. Kato didn't care, the chain could be repaired whereas the star was irreplaceable.

"Bitch!" the blonde spat at her. Kato simply gave the model a stony look and turned to walk away. It was only then that she noticed the entourage behind her. There was the designer followed by a few assistants and behind them, security who was ushering a photographer out the door. She felt ill when she recognized the face. It was the same reporter from "The Limelight" who had seemed to hound her at every turn back home. Now here she was, thousands of miles and an ocean away, with a new identity, and she still couldn't get away from him. The assistants swarmed Kato and removed the precious dress from her before any damage could be done to it. She could see the designer himself going meticulously over the dress, checking for any damage. Kato didn't care if she had to pay him every cent the garment was worth, she got what was important and she'd pay any price for it. Her thoughts went back to the photographer. Although security had been quick to remove him, she had the sinking feeling that he had gotten what he wanted and that the damage had been done.

***

It couldn't have looked worse. The front page photo had captured Kato just as her clenched fist had yanked the star from the blonde's neck. And if that wasn't bad enough, from the angle of the shot, it looked like Kato had just punched the other model, her head tilted back from the force. Kato cringed as she read the headline, *Cat Fight Breaks Out on Catwalk*. She forced herself to read on: *You've heard of a "dog eat dog world", but in the world of high fashion the cats are trying to claw their way to the top. New on the scene is Kato, who has already shown her claws.*

Kato didn't even bother reading the rest of the article. She looked again at the photo. She certainly hadn't gotten off to a good start in her new career. She was going to get a bad rap and nobody was going to want to work with her. Thank goodness she already had some magazine deals lined up.

***

You just couldn't get better advertising for free. The large colour photograph on the front page of "The Limelight" shot Donald Steele's designer dress to instant fame. They couldn't keep up with the orders that were coming in. First irritated with the model that had caused such a scene, Donald had a change of heart. He scanned the article again. Kato. He took note of the name.

***

Why had he volunteered to do this Viktor thought. Disposable diapers, baby powder, bread, eggs, that was the last of the things on the list Susan had given him. He cursed Rod, Susan's husband who was out of town on business yet again. As he stood in line at the check-out counter with the shopping cart of items, he brushed his thick dark brown hair out of his eyes. It was cut fairly short in back, but was left longer in front. Although it was brushed to the one side, it tended to fall into his one eye, and it always seemed to happen whenever his hands were full.

With his vision now totally clear, a rack of magazines caught his eye. He scanned the covers, looking for something to hold his interest, and boy, did it ever! Viktor picked up the copy of "The Limelight" and studied the photo on the front page. Even by the side profile he could tell it was her. Skimming through the article, Viktor felt disbelief. When he had met Kato at the Christmas party he had gotten good vibes from her, but his judgment must have been way off because it looked like she turned out to be a first-class bitch. Despite his feelings he found himself adding "The Limelight" to the pile of items to be rung in.

***

It was a dizzying pace. Kato's head hadn't stopped spinning since her return to American soil. First it was a shoot for "Bleu Chat", one of the top fashion magazines in the country. They had wanted her face on the cover and, so it seemed, did everyone else. Kato had ended up on half-a-dozen magazines in the past few months. She took a moment now to look at their covers. There was her in a navel baring dress, another of her in a wet swimsuit, her hair also wet and slicked back. It made her shiver to think about that one. She put the magazines aside when the phone rang.

An interview? Kato was at a loss. With all the attention she had been getting of late she should have anticipated that at some point someone was going to want to interview her. Fortunately her tight schedule saved her for the time being. She was going to be flying to Italy for some fashion shows and then once back home would be tied up with shoots for a cosmetic company. She gave her excuses, hung up and then let out a sigh of relief. But it made her think. What could she tell the press? If her true identity became known, then she could no longer pass herself off as being of Asian origin, one of the reasons for her current success.

But if she fabricated a story, the media would be sure to check into it and discover that Kato had no past. She wondered how much longer she could keep up the pretense before the truth came out.

***

Derrick Wade looked at his latest masterpiece. Well, that's what he liked to call them. He had been with "The Limelight" for just over four years and had made a name for himself by always being at the right place at the right time. He looked at his latest victim. Kato. Who was she? She seemed to have come out of nowhere. He studied the photo closely. She sure was a beauty, her looks were almost too perfect. Derrick's eyes narrowed. Plastic surgery? He picked up a note pad from a nearby table and made a note to himself. This was something he was going to have to check into.

***

Everywhere Viktor turned, there she was. It was like she had set out to haunt him. He picked up the glossy magazine and didn't know what to look at first, her beautiful face, or her exquisite body. He took the magazine to the check-out counter and pulled out his wallet. It was just one more magazine featuring her on the cover to add to his growing pile.

***

Kato took a deep breath and raised her face to the sky. The early morning air was fresh as she headed off for her daily jog along the beach with Brutus by her side. He would keep pace with her once in a while, but then take off fast after a bird or whatever distracted him on any particular day. That's what he was doing now and his absence gave her mind a chance to wander.

Kato thought of the conversation she had the previous evening with Toma. He had told her that even though she was financially independent, that she was still welcome to stay in his home. She had accepted his offer for the time being. With her full schedule she didn't feel that it was fair to Brutus to have to put him in a kennel while she was away on travel. She was also thinking of herself, Toma was the closest thing she had to family.

She saw Brutus heading towards her and she stopped to pick up a stick. She tossed in the air and laughed as he jumped high in the air. What he lacked in grace he made up for in determination. She called him and he trotted up to her, dropping the stick at her feet. She knelt down to pat his head and was startled by his low growl. His body became taunt as he stared straight ahead. Kato turned around to see what he was so intense about, grabbing his collar at the same time. She thought she had seen a tall figure go behind a garage of a nearby house but she couldn't be sure. She could feel Brutus pulling on his collar, trying to break free in order to pursue his foe, either real or imagined. She led

Brutus in the direction of home, relieved that he was there by her side.

Chapter 11

Italy! Kato was excited as the plane touched down. Her last visit overseas had been rushed, with no chance to see any of the sights. She was determined to make sure this time was different. The fashion show was taking place in Milan, but once that was done she had two weeks all to herself. Her personal agenda included a trip to Florence and then on to Naples. She was also hoping to visit at least one vineyard. She smiled to herself, she just might become a connoisseur of wine yet.

***

Kato was relieved to note that the model with the cascading blonde hair was absent from this particular show. Kato instinctively put her hand to her throat even though she knew there would be no star there. She had made a point of leaving it in a safe place. Much to her relief the fashion show went off without any disasters.

Back at her hotel room Kato headed straight to her suitcase and pulled out a velvet-lined box. She raised the lid, lifted the sparkling star out of the box and fastened the chain around her neck. Her work was done and her time was her own to spend however she wished. Her vacation had officially started.

***

Once in Florence Kato did the usual tourist things. She visited the Pitti Palace and the Uffize Palace, two well-known museums. She sampled the local food, and checked out the shops. Being in Italy she made a point of checking out the shoe stores. Boy, did she ever check out the shoe stores, she ended up with eight pairs in all. Her favourite pair was the gold-tone sandals, the straps made from the softest kid leather. They would be perfect with the peacock dress she had made famous. After its profound success the designer had insisted on presenting one to Kato. Although it was beautiful she couldn't see herself in anything quite so elaborate, but she hadn't dared turn down such a gift and risk insulting him. Maybe she would wear the dress after all. She closed her suitcase decisively. Next stop, Naples.

***

More food and more shopping. After two days in Naples Kato had to admit she was ready for something new. Yet here she was gazing through the window of yet another shoe store. Cole spotted her from across the street. Her back was towards him, yet even before he saw her face he knew she was going to be stunning. She simply had the stature and poise of a beautiful woman. A few car horns honked at him as he dodged the traffic but he ignored their angry sounds. He was on a mission.

Kato heard a commotion behind her and swung around just in time to see a tall slim man artfully dodge a speeding car. His momentum continued and Kato took a step back as he stopped just inches in front of her. She clutched her purse close to her as he made another swift movement.

Cole took a couple of steps back and apologized for his forwardness. Kato felt herself relaxing and even managed a weak smile and managed, "That's okay, no harm done." She was about to walk away when he offered to buy her a coffee and motioned to a nearby restaurant. Why not Kato thought, it was a very public place, she should be safe enough. Also, she was at the point where she had just about had enough of her own company. She took him up on his offer.

He introduced himself as Colosimo, but asked that she call him Cole. He told her that he spent his time overseeing a family-owned vineyard. He was separated and had two sons, aged four and two. She told him briefly about herself, filling him in only on her present situation. They sat in the restaurant for quite some time talking about this and that. When it became apparent that they still had more they wanted to talk about they decided to stay and order a late lunch.

Cole had ordered a bottle of wine for them to share, one from his own vineyard of course. By the time the pizza was served she had become quite hungry and reached gingerly for a slice.

Cole had watched her throughout the meal and had to admire the way she attacked her food with such zest. He was so sick of the way most women seemed to just pick at their food. Of course, most women probably weren't blessed with the amazing metabolism Kato seemed to possess. He had also taken note of her face, the warm wonderful eyes, her smooth glowing skin, and her wonderful smile. And when she laughed, it was like he had become mesmerized.

The waiter brought over some fresh fruit, a reminder that their time together was coming to an end. Impulsively Cole extended an invitation to her to visit his vineyard. Kato accepted and wrote down the name and address of the hotel she was staying at on a napkin and handed it to him. They agreed that he would pick her up at eleven o'clock the next morning.

Once they parted Kato began to have her doubts. Two kids. It wasn't that she didn't like kids, but something Karen had told her came to mind. Karen had gone out with someone who had a child, but she had broken it off because it wasn't working out. She remembered Karen's words, "When you're with someone with kids, it's never an equal relationship. The one with the kids is always going to call the shots. You begin to feel like a second class citizen, or worse yet, invisible."

As Kato reached the hotel she tried to put those thoughts out of her head. She would be going back home in less than a week so it wasn't likely that they would ever be in a relationship anyhow.

***

True to his word Cole had pulled up to the hotel at eleven o'clock sharp. It was a beautiful day and Kato had been waiting outside the lobby for him, so the moment he pulled up they were on their way. On his way to the hotel Cole had been trying to figure out how he should approach this young woman, and young she was, ten years younger than him to be exact. Would she be interested in him romantically? He had to look at the reality of it, two young kids are a lot of baggage when you're trying to get back into the dating game.

They had arrived at the vineyard and Kato took off her sunglasses to survey the lush greenery that surrounded her, but quickly put them back on as the combination of the bright sunshine and brilliant colours hurt her eyes. A woman with graying hair came out of the house and started towards them. There was a young child in her arms and another following close behind her.

Cole was still holding Kato's hand from when he had helped her out of the car. They disengaged their hands as Cole took the infant from the older woman's arms, but not before cold black eyes had spotted the gesture of intimacy. Cole made the introductions. The woman was his mother, and the child he was holding was his youngest son Antonio. As Cole introduced his older son Enzo, the child eyed her suspiciously as he clung to one of his father's legs. He wasn't the only one to give her the evil eye, Cole's mother was darting dark looks at her.

"Where's father?" Cole asked his mother. She answered, "He's gone to spend some time at the neighbour's. He said he would be back in time for dinner." was the clipped reply. Cole had another more pressing question, "Why are the children here today?" "Angelina decided that she didn't want them today, have fun!" his mother said sarcastically as she abruptly turned away and walked towards the house. Cole reached down with his free hand to grasp one of Enzo's hands. With his leg finally free Cole was able to move forward. He told Kato to go around to the back of the house where there was a garden, he would meet her there as soon as he put the children down for a nap. That suited Kato just fine, she had no wish to spend any more time than she had to with such a rude woman.

Quite a bit of time had passed before she saw Cole round the corner of the house and when he did he wasn't alone. Clinging to one of his pant legs was Enzo. "He didn't want a nap." explained Cole. Kato could see that her tour of the vineyard was not going to happen. Instead, the afternoon consisted of Cole playing various games with Enzo. Kato was more than willing to join in, but whenever she tried to be a part of the activities, Enzo would have no part of it. He would either begin to cry or throw a temper tantrum. Kato gave up and walked around the garden until she came to a quiet shady corner. A bench had been strategically placed under the shade of a tree and there she sat.

Kato could hear voices near the house, and then she saw Cole motioning for her to come. It was time for dinner. She welcomed the coolness of the interior of the house. Inside she was introduced to Cole's father. Where his mother's eyes were cold and hard, his were warm and welcoming. Well at least one person in Cole's family didn't hate her.

Once they were seated a servant appeared with the first course, risotto, a rice dish with vegetables. They all bowed their heads and Kato followed suit as Cole's father said grace. The only conversation that took place during the first course was between Cole and his father. Kato would normally try to carry on a polite conversation with her hostess but decided to not waste the energy. The next course consisted of pasta covered with a thick chunky meat sauce that was a little more spicy than what she was used to, and she ended up drinking more wine than she had intended. She didn't care. The only person who noticed was Cole's mother, and she was already disgusted with Kato, so what the heck.

The room became silent as the next course was served. The servant had placed a plate, with a pork chop on each one, in front of everyone but Kato. Kato could see the servant was feeling very uncomfortable, and almost slinked out of the room. Cole's mother said in a clear, concise voice, "You must forgive us, your arrival was on short notice, and we didn't have time to go to the market." Kato managed to give her a tight smile. Cole remained silent. He knew that the fridge was well-stocked, and even if it hadn't been, the cook could easily have taken the largest cut of meat and split it into two. What was his mother playing at?

Cole's father spoke, "Kato, please accept my serving." Kato replied, "I'm really not that hungry, but thank you for the offer." "As you wish." he replied and started to cut into the meat, but not before he threw a disapproving glance at his wife. The look was lost on her however as she seemed to be studying the end of her fork.

The men continued their conversation and Kato found herself studying Cole. She had just lost respect for him. He should have been the one to jump in, offering and insisting she take his portion. She had a feeling that once she was gone he wouldn't even call his mother on it.

It seemed an eternity before the dessert was served. A large bowl of fruit was placed on the table for everyone to help themselves but Kato didn't partake. True to her word, she no longer had an appetite.

After the meal Kato asked Cole to drive her back to the hotel. They were just about to leave when they heard an ear-piercing scream. It seemed Enzo wanted to come along. Kato resigned herself to sitting in the back seat. It was just as well, Cole would have to give all his attention to Enzo, thereby relieving her of having to carry on a conversation with Cole. She found she no longer had anything to say to him.

On the journey to the hotel, Kato thought of how Cole let others rule his life. She could see how, even at the age of four, Enzo knew just how to manipulate his father to get his own way and have his father to himself. If a woman did manage to get close to Cole despite his son's efforts to the contrary they would still have to get past his over-protective and conniving mother. Kato began to pity Cole. If he didn't find his backbone soon she could see a long, lonely future stretching out in front of him.

The car hadn't even come to a full stop before Kato started to open the door to get out. It was a brief good-bye. There wasn't any need for words, the child sitting defiantly beside Cole said it all. Kato walked through the entrance of the hotel and never looked back, physically or metaphorically. She had gotten a taste of what Karen had been talking about regarding relationships with single parents and it had left a bad taste in her mouth. Not wanting to give all men that were single parents a bad rap, she decided to put this bad experience down to Cole's spinelessness. She decided she had enough of Italy and once in her hotel room she began to pack. She was going home.

***

Kato hadn't called Toma to let him know that she was returning early, she would just surprise him. Unfortunately that meant trying to get a taxi, not an easy feat at a busy airport. She was ready to give up and call Toma when a taxi driver got part way out of his taxi to call out to her, "Hey lady! Got someone here that doesn't mind sharing, how 'bout it?" Kato dragged her luggage to the back of the taxi. While the driver loaded her suitcases in the trunk, she got into the back seat. She turned to thank the other fare, but could only manage one word, "Hi."

The man was massive. He must have been close to seven feet tall and every inch of his frame was muscle. His brown hair was cut in a military-style crew cut and he would have been quite intimidating had it not been for his wide, friendly grin. He extended a huge paw, "The name is Max, better known as Max the Machine." Kato looked blankly back at him. He continued, "I take it you're not a fan of professional wrestling?" She was just about to answer when the taxi driver sat behind the wheel and asked, "Where to?" Max turned to Kato, "I don't know if there's someone you're rushing home to, but I'm not. I'd really like for you to join me for dinner." Max could see she was hesitant, "Just as friends of course, no strings attached." She debated. Toma would have finished dinner by now and she didn't feel like scrounging around for leftovers so she decided to accept his offer.

He gave the address to the hotel he was staying at and they were on their way. Impressive Kato thought as they pulled up in front of the hotel. Professional wrestling must be a lucrative business. Their luggage was unloaded and Max effortlessly picked all of it up and took it to the front desk. He instructed them to hold the luggage there until they finished their meal and then they went to the dining room where they were seated immediately. It seemed Mr. Machine had some pull around here.

Max turned out to be a witty and fun dinner companion. Kato found that once she looked past his massive size, he was just an ordinary guy. She had expected to pay for her own meal, but Max had taken care of the bill before she could even protest. They exited the dining room and Max retrieved all of their luggage from the front desk.

"I thought maybe you'd come up for awhile." Max said persuasively. Kato politely declined. She saw that her response did not please him. In an angry voice he accused her of being a tease and went on to say that after buying her such an expensive meal that he expected something from her in return. Kato was stunned. Where did this come from all of a sudden? She didn't know if it was because the last couple of experiences she had with men had turned so sour, but she suddenly felt the anger rise up in her and it came to the surface. She opened her purse and whipped out her wallet, "Fine! You think I owe you? Tell me, how much did my meal come to? I'll pay you back every cent!" Kato pulled out a wad of money and waved it in his face and continued to yell at him, "Better yet, how about if I pay for *your* meal too, that way *you* can owe *me*!"

Max looked at the woman in front of him and was dumbfounded, and then became sheepish as she made him see what a jerk he had just been. He then felt a great deal of admiration and respect for her. He apologized profusely and insisted that she keep her money. He hailed her a taxi and loaded her suitcases in himself. He then handed the driver a large amount of currency and told him, "Take the lady wherever she wants to go, and take good care of her." He then took one of his business cards, wrote his personal cell phone number on the back and handed it to Kato, "If there's anything I can ever do for you, don't hesitate to call."

Kato gave the driver her address and then and sank back in the seat. It was going to feel so good to finally be home.

Chapter 12

"Damn!" Carlyle Douglas slammed his fist onto the highly polished desk. His latest film had been a dud. He should never had let himself be talked into backing such a lame excuse of a movie. In the past, coming of age flicks had done quite well at the box office, but this particular one lacked any kind of story line. The acting in it had sucked too. He would never hire that useless Veronica Sutton again, nothing but attitude and getting to the set late every day. His suspicion was that she had gotten herself into drugs.

Carlyle's thoughts continued. He needed something up-to-date. What was hot right now? Action! But not just guns and explosions, he wanted suspense, drama, intrigue! He wanted it all! He looked down to where his fist had hit the desk. Just to the right of the spot he had hit was a screenplay that had been sent to him the week before. He had been sitting on the answer to his dilemma all this time. He had skimmed through it the other day and recalled that the main male character was a man trained in martial arts. In it were stunts, car chases, espionage, even humour and romance. The number of actors that would be able to play the male lead would be limited, not many had martial arts skills. The female lead was going to be even harder to fill. It would have to be someone athletic, lean and preferably Asian. The martial arts experience wasn't so important, the few fighting scenes the female lead had were few and could easily be taught to her.

Think! Think! Who could he get? Carlyle thought of a couple of actresses but quickly dismissed them. He wanted someone who hadn't been type-cast. He wanted someone new. He wanted... *her*!

Carlyle picked up the copy of "The Limelight" that had been delivered to him a while ago. He rarely read through them, but received every issue as he was a shareholder. This particular cover showed a woman, looking to be Asian having a go at another woman. Well it looked like she would have no objections to the fight scenes. He read through the article. Hmm, she was a model, but that didn't deter him, lots of models had made the transition to acting. Promoting that angle could even prove to be a positive box office draw. He kept reading. Ah, there it was, her name was Kato.

Carlyle buzzed Miss Templeton, "Get me everything you can find on this new model Kato... no... it's just the one name... and one more thing... find her for me too." He then leaned back in his chair, hands on the back of his head and said to himself out loud in a self-satisfied voice, "You really are a genius!"

***

Carlyle Douglas wants her? Well of course he didn't want her, Cassandra Carrington, he wanted a woman called Kato. She found it ironic. After her mother's death, she couldn't even make it onto the grounds of his studio and now he was welcoming her with open arms and a great leading role. Her first impulse was to tell him to go to hell but she thought twice. It was a good opportunity and acting really was her first love. She touched the star that hung around her neck. She was going to do it, and she was going to shine!

***

Veronica Sutton glared at the magazine cover. So this was the bitch that was getting the next leading role. Some people didn't know their place. What would an air-head model know about acting? Veronica decided that she was going to watch this one real close, and when she fell flat on her face, Veronica was going to be there to keep her down. But in the meantime she had a more pressing issue. She grabbed her phone and called her drug dealer. She told herself she would quit the drugs once she got her weight down to where she wanted it. She had felt the pressure put on her to lose weight when she was acting in her last movie. The camera really did add ten pounds.

***

Carlyle had to admit that it took a lot to impress him, but impressed he was. He had anticipated Kato needing a lot of coaching, but she was like a seasoned pro. Her acting ability was astounding. Carlyle took his leave, things seemed to be running smoothly without any effort by him. He had better things to do with his time.

***

Being in real estate Viktor had never really had any interest in celebrities or followed who was who, but lately he had been making an exception. It was almost like he had no choice, everywhere he turned, there was her face, and her name was on everyone's lips, Kato. Now he found himself looking at her image yet again. This entertainment magazine wasn't featuring her per say, the focus was more on the movie that was being shot that she was starring in.

Viktor was determined to get her out of his mind and turned his attention to the task at hand. He had been collaborating with another realtor on this particular deal and needed to meet with him to go over some papers. He decided to take his chances that the man would be home.

He looked towards the house and noticed that there were quite a few lights on. Good. At least he wouldn't be getting anyone out of bed. He rang the doorbell and didn't have to wait very long before he heard a woman's voice, "I'll get it!" The voice was followed by the barking of a dog, a *big* dog! He prepared himself for flight. What he wasn't prepared for was the sight he saw once the door opened. The danger wasn't in the Doberman that was being restrained by its collar, the danger was the brilliant green cat-like eyes that stared back at him. It was *her*!

Viktor found his voice, "Uh, is Toma in?" Kato had had a shock of her own when she opened the door and said awkwardly, "Uh, yes, please come in." She pulled Brutus away, "I'll put him in the kitchen if you like." "I'd appreciate that." Viktor replied. He watched her walk away and couldn't help but notice the way her skin-tight jeans showed off her butt. He quickly averted his eyes only to see a portrait of her. No, the clothing was all wrong, too old-fashioned. This must have been her mother. The resemblance was certainly there. Odd, he knew Toma had been married, but he always thought that they had been childless. Toma Kato. Kato. It was all starting to make sense, sort of.

Toma came to the door and the two men shook hands then Toma led him to the study where they got right down to business. They poured over the papers for well over an hour after which they got all the details sorted out and the deal firmed up. With business out of the way, Viktor was taking his leave, "I'll be going now, I hope I didn't disrupt any plans you may have had with your daughter." Viktor felt foolish the moment he uttered the words, it was probably obvious that he was fishing for information.

"Not at all," Toma responded, "and she's not my daughter." The men said their good-byes and Viktor left, more curious than ever. Not his daughter, he mused. Then what? She wasn't his wife, she had passed away a few years ago. Then who? His lover? But what were the odds that he found someone who so resembled his dead wife? He decided he was going to find out the answer.

***

Toma closed the door behind Viktor and smiled to himself. He knew that the reply he had given Viktor was not what he had expected or wanted to hear. He wasn't trying to mislead Viktor, but if Viktor wanted to know more, then he was going to have to go to the source, Kato. Toma left it up to her as to who she wanted to tell her circumstances to.

***

With Kato throwing herself into her work she had almost been able to get Viktor out of her mind, but then, out of the blue there he was right in the forefront of her thoughts. She thought about how he had reacted to seeing her at the door, the way he had recoiled. Well, if he was like everyone else, he would have read the tabloid and probably thinks of her as a psycho bitch from hell. It shouldn't have mattered to her what one person's opinion of her was, but it did, and it hurt.

***

Could it be fate? Viktor hung up and looked up at the ceiling of his office. That was a call from one of the cast members of "Dragon of Danger", the very film that Kato was working on. One of the actors was looking to locate permanently to the area and wanted Viktor as his realtor. He had a legitimate reason to come and go on the movie set. The question was, would he take advantage of it?

***

Well, it was out of his hands. Viktor had been asked to drop some listings off at the set. Originally his client was supposed to stop by his office but he was delayed on the set and wanted Viktor to meet him at the movie set. The shooting was taking place on the studio grounds and Viktor was stopped at the front gate where he gave his name and was told to proceed.

No one even noticed Viktor as he approached the set. The crew was concentrating on doing their respective jobs and all others were mesmerized by the scene unfolding before them. As Viktor watched he got caught up in the action taking place. It seemed so real. Damn she was good! And hot! He found the black leather outfit that fit her like a second skin and hugged her every curve incredibly sexy.

"Cut!" yelled the director. The spell was broken and Viktor came back to reality. He stopped a crew member and inquired as to where he could find Ross Tait, then headed off in the direction the crew member had pointed in.

***

After the camera had stopped rolling and the crew dispersed Kato let herself collapse onto the floor. It had been a long, grueling day and her muscles were really feeling it. Jon Wong, the lead male actor, had come to know Kato quite well and he could see that she was all done in. He came over to where she sat and started massaging her shoulders. It felt like heaven and Kato closed her eyes and let his fingers work their magic.

***

Viktor's business was finally done and he debated on whether or not to seek out Kato to at least say hello. He was heading back to the spot where the scene had taken place but stopped short when he caught sight of her, and *him*. It seemed to Viktor that the last thing the couple would appreciate was an interruption. He turned on his heel and left.

***

Derrick Wade was baffled. He wasn't used to coming up against brick walls, but this time he had come to a dead end after exhausting all of his resources. It was as if this Kato didn't exist. His eyes narrowed. Maybe she didn't. He had been looking for a person named Kato and various versions of the name, but what if it wasn't her real name? Because of her height he guessed that maybe she was only part Asian. That opened up endless possibilities when it came to surnames. He was like a dog with a bone, more determined than ever to get answers. Actually more like a bloodhound, he wouldn't stop until he had tracked down all of her secrets.

***

Viktor finished his warm-up exercises and started his jog along the beach. The weather forecast was calling for a sweltering hot day and he set out early to beat the heat. He adjusted the volume on his iPod before picking up the pace.

***

"Brutus!" yelled Kato. Now where had he taken off to? She continued on her jog. She wasn't concerned about his absence; he always showed up eventually. She turned her attention to the sky. There wasn't a cloud in it, and she could already feel the heat of the sun on her shoulders. She was about to head to the water's edge when she was knocked forward onto the sand. She cried out in pain as her arm was twisted behind her back. The pain was forgotten as she felt the sharp edge of the knife against her throat. The nightmare from her past had come back to haunt her! It all seemed surreal, and Kato could feel herself blacking out.

A low guttural growl sounded in the attacker's ear. He jumped back, dropping the knife. He backed away slowly and once he realized that the Doberman was going to stand guard over the woman rather than attack him, he turned and ran.

Kato watched the man flee. Brutus laid down on the sand beside her, whimpering softly. "Oh Brutus!" she cried as she wrapped her arms around him. She hugged him tight as she buried her face in his fur, then her body began to shake.

It had taken Viktor a while to realize what had been happening. He had been lost in his own thoughts, listening to the music on his iPod. He had been quite a distance away when the situation hit him and he broke out in a full run. He saw the attacker run off and was tempted to take chase, but concern for the victim made him curb his desire to catch the bastard. He continued towards the woman.

Two things made Viktor stop dead in his tracks. The dog that had gotten up from the sand and that was now standing, growling at him. The second thing was the woman. It was her! He saw her shaking and decided to take his chances. He dropped to his knees, hoping the dog would cease to see him as a threat. "Are you okay?" he asked softly. Kato had looked up when she heard Brutus' growls but in her state of shock it didn't register with her who it was. She only heard the soothing voice and her instincts told her she was safe with this man. She called Brutus to her side. Brutus came and sat quietly beside her, but still remained on guard.

Viktor saw her eyes as she looked up at him. Those mesmerizing eyes looked at him but they had a blank look to them. In her state of shock she didn't even recognize him. She was still shaking and he gently took her arm and helped her up from the sand. Slowly Viktor started to guide her home.

Kato was finally coming out of the shock only to feel shocked again when she realized who was walking beside her, Viktor Cross! She suddenly felt embarrassed. What could he be thinking of her? She stayed silent until they reached the front door of Toma's house and then thanked him for his help. Viktor replied, "No problem. Are you going to be okay?" Kato knelt down and gave Brutus a hug and a pat, "Yes, I'll be fine, thanks. It's quite hot, did you want to come in and have a drink?" Viktor hesitated for only a moment before accepting her offer.

The hours flew by as they talked. Viktor told her about himself, how his parents had both passed away in a boating accident when he was nineteen and his sister

Susan was twenty-one. Both he and his sister were working at their family-owned real estate office at the time and kept the business going. A few years later Susan got married and wanted out of the business, so Viktor had been keeping it going ever since, eventually buying her out.

Kato opened up to Viktor, but only so much, telling him as much about herself as she dared. As the conversation wore on, Viktor became even more intrigued with the woman before him, the woman with the bewitching green eyes that she hid behind brown contacts. The more she said about herself, the more questions he seemed to have, but didn't dare voice. One thing he knew for sure, he had to see her again.

Viktor looked at his watch. He really did need to be going. Think Viktor think. What excuse could he make to see her again? Running! It would be the perfect way to be close to her, get to know her better *and* he could ensure her safety. He didn't know why he felt so protective towards her, maybe because he had seen this vulnerable side of her. It made him feel like something had physically gripped his heart. He broached the subject of running with her and she agreed. He felt that he had somehow accomplished a mission, and with that settled he took his leave.

***

There it was. Viktor had hoped that the man wouldn't come back for it. He took his sweatshirt that he had tied around his shoulders earlier and with great care used it to pick up the knife that lay half-buried in the sand.

***

It always seemed an eternity between her jogs with Viktor, and yet, the time they spent together just flew. They didn't talk much during their runs, but they would make up for it afterward. Sometimes they would head to a restaurant for a casual meal, or simply sit and talk on the beach, enjoying the sunset. This was one such night.

Kato was moving her lips, and Viktor knew she was talking and that he should be listening, but all he could do was stare at her lips. They looked full and soft and he couldn't resist any longer. He leaned in towards her.

Kato had felt it coming. The sexual tension had been building and when he finally kissed her it was like something unleashed itself inside of her. Passion! Passion that she hadn't dared hope she could ever feel again. They were reaching a new level and Kato had to stop. It wasn't that she didn't want to continue, but she couldn't. Not until she told Viktor the whole truth about herself. Her past, who she was, and how she became who she is now.

***

Viktor listened, trying to let it all sink in. Her childhood, her mother's death, her relationship with the man who had left her for dead. It certainly explained why she had reacted so strongly after her ordeal on the beach. The terror, the pain and the suffering must have all come crashing back. She went on to tell him about Toma's role in her life including his gift to her and why he had given it to her. Viktor had wondered about the diamond star that she always wore, now he knew why she was never without it. She also explained about the incriminating photo on the front page of "The Limelight" and how it had, ironically, helped get her to where she was today.

Viktor was speechless. He looked at this woman before him. She had gone through so much, and he realized how hard it must have been for her to tell him all this, how much she had put her trust in him, revealing her true identity. He vowed he would never betray that trust. Words couldn't express what he felt at that moment. He took her in his arms, not letting go until the night turned to dawn.

Chapter 13

The time had finally come! Kato stepped out of the limousine, followed by Viktor. They both had to shield their eyes from the blinding lights of the camera flashbulbs. It had been a long time in coming, what with the delays in editing and even some of the scenes being re-shot, but the premier showing of "Dragon of Danger" was now a reality. The studio had been working day and night to make the pre-Christmas deadline, but here it was, February of 2010.

As Kato walked towards the entrance she couldn't help but notice that her outfit was causing a sensation. She was wearing a short, tight-fitting black leather dress. Over the dress she wore an unbuttoned ankle-length black leather coat. It wasn't her choice, but Carlyle Douglas had insisted on it. It had been delivered to her home a week ago. At first she was going to refuse to wear it, but then thought twice. It did suit the lean, mean image of the character she portrayed in the movie, and it would be a good idea to preserve the image as there was already talk of a sequel. No, she had let Mr. Douglas have his way this time, but only because it suited her own agenda.

Viktor was feeling extremely uneasy. He hadn't mentioned it to Kato, but he had taken the knife that her attacker on the beach had left behind and had brought it to the police. They had found fingerprints on it and they matched with a convicted criminal, Charles James, who was known for targeting celebrities. He had been released a couple of years earlier after serving his time. The police thought that he might surface at this public event, and they wanted to use this occasion to flush him out. Viktor had been uncomfortable with the idea, but was assured that there would be several plain-clothes police officers integrated into the crowd.

Viktor tackled Kato to the ground and used his body to shield her when he heard the gun shot. Screams were heard throughout the crowd and panic ensued. Flashbulbs flashed, blinding the people that were scattering in all directions, bumping into and jostling each other in their efforts to flee.

As quickly as Viktor had knocked Kato to the ground, he now swept her up so that she wouldn't get trampled. He was holding her tight as he saw heading towards them two men escorting a third man in handcuffs. "Figured you'd want to know that we got him." said one of the plain-clothed police officers, "We noticed him just as he was ready to shoot and managed to grab his arm to redirect the shot, so no harm done." The officers moved on with the man but not before the man in handcuffs glared at her with hatred and spat, "This is all your fault bitch!"

***

It was an instant hit. Of course the shooting beforehand had helped to heighten the excitement of the whole movie-going experience and the people coming out of the show were pumped. "Dragon of Danger" was on everyone's lips.

***

Kato and Viktor retired to his house for the remainder of the evening, the house that he lived in that is, he owned several properties. Viktor was still shaken at the thought of almost losing Kato, while she was deeply touched at how he had risked his own life to save hers. Emotions ran high in both of them, and although their love-making was always passionate, tonight there was an extra edge. It went on and on, neither one of them wanting to fully let go, not wanting it to end. But finally they could stand it no more, they had to give in to the passion that consumed them. When the moment hit, the force of her orgasm consumed her entire body. Exhausted, she let her body fall forward, laying motionless on top of Viktor. Viktor wrapped his arms around her and held her tight, he didn't even pull out of her. He never wanted to let her go.

They stayed like that for some time, and then she felt it, growing inside of her. The sensation made her come alive and she couldn't tell if it was her, or Viktor's enlarging penis that started to throb. All she knew was that her body had to respond to it.

Viktor let out a moan. He had thought it was a dream, but his eyes were open, and there she was, moving to her own rhythm, making him want her all over again. His body started moving, matching her motion for motion, faster and faster, until they both couldn't take it anymore. Viktor took her hips in his hands and thrust even deeper inside her. They were both satisfied at last.

As Viktor pulled Kato towards him, he brought her far enough up that he was no longer inside her. It had been fantastic, but there was only so much one man could take.

***

He was back. Fraser had to admit that it felt great to be back on American soil. He had been away longer than he had wished, but he had wanted to make sure that enough time had passed that the police would have all but given up on solving Cassandra Carrington's murder. The coast seemed to be clear and Fraser claimed his luggage and then was on his way.

"Hello! Anyone home?" Fraser yelled out as he came through the front door of his parent's home. Charlotte Douglas jumped. She had all but given up on her son coming home but here he was. She had to admit that she had mixed feelings about his return. With him gone, she was able to keep her head buried in the sand, but now, well, she had to know the truth. She reached into the top drawer of her dresser and pulled out the clipping. She put it into the pocket of her cardigan then headed down the stairs.

"Mother!" As Fraser watched his mother coming down the few remaining stairs he thought that something wasn't quite right, and it wasn't because she had a cast on one leg and was walking with a cane. His mother, usually pleased to see him, especially after such a long absence, was unusually subdued. She gave him a quiet "Hello Fraser." then motioned for him to follow her into the living room and sit down on a sofa. She sat down beside him, then pulled out the newspaper clipping from her pocket and handed it to him.

Fraser was puzzled as he took the clipping and started to read through the short article. Charlotte watched his face as he read it. Even though he was quite tanned, she could see how his face paled as he read it. He dropped the clipping and put his head in his hands. She knew. Even from the sketchy article and no mention of him in it, she had figured it out.

The underlying tension that had been with him ever since that night came to the surface and he broke down, confessing all. Charlotte was in a state of shock. Even though she had suspected it all along, deep down, she had always hoped she was mistaken. But there it was in front of her, the ugly truth. She was at a loss. She couldn't turn her own son in to the police, and besides, Fraser going to prison wouldn't bring the young woman back. Best to leave things as they were.

***

Viktor pointed at a ring in the showcase, "Let me see that one over there." He was exhausted, he felt like he had been in every jewelry store in all of California. His energy returned when he finally found what he had been looking for. He took the ring from the sales clerk's hand. The band was platinum, and the emerald-cut two carat stone reminded Viktor of her eyes. He had thought of a conventional diamond for her engagement ring but somehow nothing but an emerald would do, "Perfect, I'll take it!"

Viktor knew which night he was going to pop the question. They were to attend a party that Carlyle Douglas was throwing to celebrate the large opening day box office numbers of "Dragon of Danger". That night there was also going to be the announcement of a sequel. The party was being held on Valentine's Day, and Viktor had already made reservations at a restaurant for a late dinner for two. He would ask her then!

***

Kato had decided on a crimson red outfit. The skirt was long and straight but had a high slit up one side. The matching top was simple with a scoop neck, but was cropped short and showed an expanse of her lean, muscular abdomen. She made a point of getting ready before Viktor showed up. She wanted a chance to speak with Toma, hoping to convince him to come along. He had declined her invitation, as well as the one to the premier of "Dragon of Danger". He seemed to be withdrawing, keeping more to himself, and she was worried. Even Brutus didn't seem himself, getting easily irritated and snappish.

Kato searched the house. She couldn't find either of them and finally checked the kitchen. She should have done that first as there was a note on the fridge from Toma that said he was taking Brutus for a walk. It was almost like he knew she was going to try to convince him to go. Well no chance of that now. The doorbell rang, it was time to go.

Kato opened the door and let out a cry of surprise when she saw Viktor, holding a bouquet of two dozen long stemmed red roses. Even before taking them, she threw herself into his arms.

***

They showed up fashionably late for the party that was being held at the Douglas residence. Kato thought again of the irony, Carlyle Douglas not only welcoming her into his home, but also throwing a party in her honour.

It wasn't too long into the evening before Carlyle made his speech, giving the latest numbers at the box office, and making the big announcement of a sequel. His speech was followed by thunderous applause.

The party wore on and Kato was about to suggest to Viktor that they leave. They had just gotten to the front door when she heard Carlyle said to her, "Kato, there's someone here that would like to meet you." She turned in his direction as he continued, "This is my son, Fraser, but he also goes by Zack."

Kato extended her hand and then froze. Viktor had his hand on the bare part of Kato's back, and he noticed she had tense up. He watched her withdraw her hand quickly from Fraser's, and then he felt it. Where his hand was touching her skin, he could feel her break into a cold sweat. She excused herself and walked quickly out the door. Viktor excused himself from the two men and went in search of her.

Viktor found her leaning against the outside wall, doubled over. She was hyperventilating! He came over to her, taking her hand and guiding her to a nearby bench. He was at a loss as to what could have made her react that way. Maybe it wasn't what, maybe it was who. Could that man be the one from her past? The one that left her for dead? He would have been angry if he hadn't been so concerned for Kato. It looked like they would be going straight home. So much for the big plans he had for tonight.

Viktor dropped Kato off at home, making sure she got inside okay. He drove away frustrated. He felt around in his jacket pocket and pulled out the ring box. He had had such high hopes for the night. Now he would have to wait for another opportunity, but it wouldn't be any time soon as he had already committed himself to go to Nevada to check out some property. He expected to be gone a week at the very least. He thought about the way he had left Kato. He couldn't have been leaving at a worse time.

***

Kato closed the door behind her and ran. She barely made it to the bathroom in time. She fell to her knees and threw up. She started to shake. How could he stand there? He acted like he had every right to be there, enjoying himself, laughing and talking with all of those other people. He should be locked up, and the key thrown away!

Kato heard Toma in the kitchen and went downstairs to say goodnight. Brutus was in the kitchen as well and as she drew closer, she held out her hand to pat Brutus, but instead of his usual happy to see her greeting he let out a low growl. She went to come closer but Brutus lunged at her. Toma acted quickly and pulled him away, dragging him outside, all the while Brutus was still intent on trying to attack Kato.

This had been a horrible night for Kato and she just wanted it to end. She went to bed but couldn't sleep because the events of the evening kept running through her head. The promising start, the happy announcement, then Fraser. So that's who he really is, Carlyle Douglas' son! The anger rose inside of her as she thought back to that day so long ago. Then it hit her, Brutus remembered too! No wonder he went ballistic, Fraser's scent would have been on her hand. Regardless, Brutus hadn't been himself lately. Just the other day she had discussed Brutus with Toma and they had decided that Toma would take him to the vet. Toma was always the one to take him there, right from the beginning, which is why Brutus was stated as his owner at the vet's office. As much as she loved Brutus and Brutus was a faithful protector to her, she could see there was a special bond between Toma and Brutus.

***

Fraser hadn't been particularly interested in his father's latest movie, but he was interested in Kato! She was so sexy and he simply had to have her! The fact that she was with someone at the party didn't stop him from deciding to pursue her, after all, he didn't see any ring on her finger. First thing in the morning he was going to visit his father's office to get her contact information. Well, maybe he would go in the afternoon, he wanted to sleep in.

***

Why didn't they let the man shoot the fucking whore? Veronica Sutton looked at the cover of "The Limelight" one more time before crumpling it into a large wad and throwing it at the wall. This Kato was too big a threat to her and her career. With Kato in the picture nobody was noticing her. She vowed to take her down, then sat on the floor and did the line of cocaine in front of her on the coffee table.

***

Derrick Wade looked at the latest photo of Kato on the front page of "The Limelight". She certainly didn't lead a dull life, now people were trying to assassinate her. It was driving him insane! He kept coming up empty when it came to her. He had even had people get into conversations with her friends, hoping his spies might extract some information from them, but no such luck. Either they didn't know anything about her past, or they simply weren't talking. But wait, they were also all nurses, and at one particular hospital. Maybe he should look there for answers! He was about to make a call when his phone rang. It was Veronica Sutton, "Veronica, to what do I owe the pleasure?... ah, yes, Kato... Ya I want to bring her down too, in fact, I'm on it right now."

***

Looking at the vet's face Toma could tell the news was going to be bad. The vet explained, "His bones have stopped growing, but his brain hasn't. As the brain continues to grow, the pressure and pain will increase and as it does, his behaviour will become more unpredictable. There is no treatment, you'll have to have him put down." The vet went on, "You don't have to do it today, but don't put it off for too long or someone, even yourself, could get hurt." Toma left the vet's office with Brutus, and a heavy heart. It was like someone had punched him in the gut. He had raised Brutus from a young pup and had become attached to the clumsy animal. It was like he was losing a good friend.

***

Kato was worried. Toma had been gone a long time and she hoped everything had gone well at the vet's. She heard Toma come through the back way, and when he came in she could see by his expression that the news was bad. Toma had a hard time getting out the words to tell her the grim news. Kato broke down in tears.

***

Kato was in the living room and was just about to head to bed when the phone on the other side of the room rang. She quickly ran to it and picked it up hoping to hear Viktor's voice but it was Fraser. He wanted to meet her, get to know her. Kato was stunned, but quickly found her voice. She would meet with him the following evening at a quiet stretch of beach. She kept the conversation brief and once she hung up her mental anguish overwhelmed her. She went to her bedroom and sat on her bed. She curled up in a ball, rocking back and forth until she was both mentally and physically drained.

***

Kato make a point of spending the entire day with Brutus, taking him for a walk on the beach and playing with him in the back yard. His behaviour had been just fine that day, and Kato began to have doubts about the plan she was about to set in motion.

***

Kato had taken great care with her appearance that evening. She took the pale gold dress out of her closet and pulled it on over her head. She smoothed it over her body and turned to look at her reflection in the mirror. With her new face and dark hair she didn't expect Fraser to realize who she was, but she was hoping that he would recognize the dress that had been his favourite on her.

Kato began to feel sick inside. She had to move fast, before she backed out. She had set the meeting time with Fraser for midnight, that way Toma would be asleep by the time she left. She was careful to be very quiet, walking with Brutus on his leash to the back door where she grabbed the keys to the Mercedes from the hook beside the door. At the car she opened the passenger door and commanded Brutus to get in. She then sat in the driver's seat, started the car and put it into gear.

***

Fraser sat on the sand, eagerly anticipating Kato's arrival. He was intrigued. What kind of woman suggests a rendezvous at midnight on a deserted beach for a first date? He found it to be unusual, but she had been quite insistent so he had agreed to meet her there.

***

Kato stopped the car. Here they were. On the way there Brutus had started vibrating and whining. Now, with the car stopped she could see he was getting even more agitated. She grabbed his leash and guided him out the driver's side door. She had made a point of wearing low shoes as she was going to be walking on sand, and even in the low shoes she found it hard to walk as Brutus was forcefully moving forward, pulling her along.

Fraser could see her coming towards him, her and a large dog. Well this wasn't quite the evening he had in mind. She wasn't that far away from him when she stopped walking. He was puzzled. Without showing any acknowledgment that she was even aware that he was there, she turned her attention to the dog.

Brutus was snapping and growling and Kato struggled to unbuckle Brutus' collar. After she did she still held it around his neck. She looked directly at Fraser. She removed the collar completely, it was time to let go, "Goodbye Brutus." she whispered.

***

Fraser knew that dress, but where had he seen it before? Then he remembered. But it couldn't be *her*, she was dead, he had killed her! Then it came to him in a flash, she had survived, and the puppy that had survived was the one that had grown into this monstrous beast that was now charging at him, its mouth in a vicious snarl. The dog that was out for revenge. The look of recognition in Fraser's eyes turned to terror as the beast attacked.

Chapter 14

Police had been called to the gruesome scene. Even the most seasoned experienced officers found themselves feeling queasy at the sight before them. They were assuming that the Lamborghini parked up on the road belonged to what remained of the person laying on the blood-soaked sand. They were doing a check on the plate number right now, but they would be confirming the person's identity with dental records.

One investigator, Travis McNeil, surveyed the area. It was easy enough to tell at a glance what had happened, they had found the blood-stained dog just a few yards from the body, but he found it strange that the dog was also dead. Best to order an autopsy on it too. It wasn't going to be easy to get answers on this one. There had been a strong wind overnight and if there had been any additional footprints, they were now gone. There wasn't even any clue as to what direction the dog had come from.

Travis headed up to where the car was parked. He could see that they were dusting it for prints, but if it came up clean, then they would be back to square one. For all they knew, someone could have come in a separate vehicle, but there was no way of knowing for sure, the pavement wasn't telling any stories. Then again, it could have been a fluke, the unlucky bastard was just at the wrong place at the wrong time. Another scenario was that it was his own dog that had turned on him, stranger things have happened.

***

Kato lay in bed, her eyes wide open, staring blankly at the ceiling. She had gone straight to bed the night before, but hadn't slept a wink. The whole horrible night kept replaying in her mind. She though of how she had let go of Brutus and then had simply turned and walked away. At the time she had felt no emotion, not even the screams of terror had registered in her mind. Not until now.

Even though Kato hadn't killed him with her own hands, she felt like she had. But then, had he not deserved what he got? She though back to the night Fraser had ripped her apart, the agonizing pain she had felt then came flooding back to her. Not just then, the pain continued for months later. Sure, she was fine now, but only because there had been a guardian angel looking out for her, Toma. Where would she have been without his generosity? Would she even be alive today if she hadn't received the excellent medical care that she had? And the plastic surgeries. She wouldn't have been able to afford them. She could very well have ended up broke and homeless, a grotesque figure trying to keep alive on the streets.

The anger welled up inside of her again when she thought about him, fit and tanned and not giving a damn. No one would ever have suspected the rich, spoiled Fraser Douglas of such a heinous crime. If she would have tried to bring charges against him, what case would she have had? There was only her word against his. With the possibility of reasonable doubt, the justice system could have failed her, and Brutus.

Brutus. She had to wonder what was to become of him now. If the police found him, they would have to put him down. But then, it was what would have happened to him in due time. Kato shut her eyes tight. Oh Brutus! She grabbed his leather collar from her nightstand drawer and held it tightly to her.

***

His identity had been confirmed, now there was the task of telling his next of kin. The examination of the dog had also been completed and its conclusion was that it had died from a brain hemorrhage. This was an odd case indeed. Travis looked at the man's name, Fraser Douglas, son of *thee* Carlyle Douglas. His job just became more challenging.

***

Travis hadn't been sure how Carlyle Douglas was going to react to the news. Travis had expected from a man like Mr. Douglas rage, maybe outrage, but he hadn't anticipated the calm, almost blank look that came over the man's face. Had the man no feelings?

Mrs. Douglas on the other hand had given a typical reaction. He had felt for her, she looked fragile and small sitting in the overstuffed armchair, one leg propped up on an ottoman, her foot in a cast. At least with the injury she had a private nurse on hand to look after her. It didn't look like her husband was going to give her any comfort.

***

Viktor finally made it home. His business in Nevada took much longer than he had wished, but now he was back. He had originally planned to stop by to see Kato when he got back into town, but because he had taken a later flight he decided instead to head straight home and to bed. Before turning off the bedside lamp he opened the top drawer of his nightstand and grabbed the velvet covered box. He lifted the lid and looked at the ring nestled within. He would surprise her in the morning.

***

Toma had a big real estate deal he was working on and wanted to get to the office early that morning. He had thrown himself into his work to keep his thoughts away from losing his beloved Brutus. Kato had told him the other day that she had decided to take Brutus to the vet to be put down. He had been terribly upset, not only because Brutus was now gone, but because he didn't get to say goodbye.

Toma made a point of getting up early. He got dressed and headed out the door before Kato had even awakened. Having skipped breakfast, he was hungry, so on his commute he decided to stop at a convenience store for a coffee and muffin. There was a newspaper at home but he hadn't thought to take it with him. Standing in line to pay he impulsively grabbed one now. He was hoping that he might have some time in his busy day to read it.

***

Viktor awoke with a start. What the? He had heard a thump and went to the front door to investigate. Ah, the newspaper. The paperboy's throw must have been off this morning and hit the door full force. He grabbed the newspaper and went inside. He would read it while having a cup of coffee.

***

Viktor put his coffee cup down slowly. It hadn't made the front page, but it grabbed his attention nonetheless. He read the name of the victim, Fraser Douglas. He started to read the article, *Fraser Zachary Douglas, son of Carlyle and Charlotte Douglas...* he read on.

Attacked by a Doberman! This was too much of a coincidence. He thought back to the night of the party, the bizarre reaction Kato had after being introduced to Fraser. He forced himself to read on. He didn't want to believe it of her, but too much was adding up. The article stated that the dog had died of a brain hemorrhage. Viktor knew of Brutus's condition. He had to see Kato *now*!

***

Viktor went to see Kato and got the answer he was seeking, and he got it without asking one question. Kato didn't have to say a word, it was all there in her face, in those eyes. He knew, and she knew he knew. Viktor had to turn away from her. Without a word he walked out the door. Kato closed the door, leaned against it and slid down to the floor, tears streaming down her face. She had lost him.

***

Toma stared at the newspaper article, his thoughts racing through his head. Thoughts of how Kato had been acting lately, and Brutus! Kato had said she had taken Brutus to be put down, but had she? He began to put two and two together. Fraser must have been the man who had left Kato for dead. No wonder she hadn't been herself lately, she must have been going through a private hell. Toma thought back to Kato's attack, the horrible pain both physical and mental that she had endured for months. He had been there, helplessly watching her suffer as she had gone through it all. He had seen the blood-soaked bed. Toma forgot about business for the rest of the day, he went home to be with Kato.

***

Toma came through the back door and walked through the house looking for Kato. He finally found her, curled up on the floor at the front door. He knelt beside her and took her in his arms, "My poor Kato, you've been through so much."

***

It took quite a while for Kato to fall asleep that night, but once she did, the dream began. Their kisses were passionate, and their bodies, both drenched in sweat felt like silk as they brushed against one another. Kato was hot, almost feverishly so, her burning desire was such that she thought she would either burst or go out of her mind. She was ready for him and as Viktor entered her, her orgasm came in one overwhelming wave. She awoke with a groan.

It took Kato a moment to realize that it had all been just a dream. She had reached out but there was nothing but a cool expand of sheet. It was a stark contrast to the hot sweat-drenched material under her wet body. But it was more than sweat beneath her, the sheet was soaked with her own body fluids. She had heard of them but had never before experienced one, a female wet dream. So they weren't just a myth!

Kato rolled to the cool side of the bed but not before checking the time on the bedside clock. It was only midnight; she had been asleep for just an hour, an hour of bliss she thought as she recalled her dream. She closed her eyes, and her body began to heat up as she envisioned Viktor. She threw the covers aside and the night air touched her nipples like a caress. Her breathing began to deepen, and she could feel the heat beginning to rush through her body. She could almost feel Viktor's hands caressing her skin, first moving from her shoulder, down to cup the fullness of her breast, then down to her hip, moving behind until he reached her buttocks. She became lost in her thoughts, imaging the weight of his body on hers as he mounted her, thrusting, deeper each time until she screamed out in ecstasy. She opened her eyes in disbelief. She felt below her to the tell-tale wetness. Just the thought of Viktor had made her orgasm! She looked at the clock; it was just going on one o'clock. It was going to be a long, lonely night.

***

Viktor lay in bed staring at the ceiling, unable to sleep. Before he had gone to Nevada, Toma had approached him with the opportunity to buy his real estate business.

Now that Viktor was back, he finally had the chance to give it some serious thought. He wondered if Toma had told Kato of his plans. She had never made any mention of it to him. Viktor had never brought the subject up with Kato while they were together, there had always been so many other things going on.

As Viktor's thoughts turned to Kato, he tried to get them out of his head. He didn't want to think about her anymore. It was about two o'clock in the morning and he was too restless to sleep. He decided to get out of bed and go for a run.

It didn't take long for Viktor to change into his athletic wear and he was off, running down the sidewalk and heading in the direction of the beach. He got to the point where the sidewalk ended and he had to start running on the side of the road. It was shortly after he started on that part of road that it happened. The car coming up from behind had been swerving erratically for some distance and the driver didn't see Viktor until the headlights of the car picked up the reflective strips on his clothing. But then it was too late. The impact sent Viktor air-bound and he landed with a dull thump. The driver didn't think twice before driving off into the night.

***

It wasn't until dawn that a passing motorist spotted Viktor laying in a crumpled heap and called 911. From the time that he had been hit, to the time that he had been found, Viktor had been in and out of consciousness, passing out from the pain, then gaining consciousness when he awoke from the pain, and so the vicious cycle continued through the hours until his rescue.

***

Carlyle Douglas paced his office floor. Patience was not one of his virtues, and he didn't know what to do with himself now that the sequel to "Dragon of Danger" had been put on hold indefinitely, due to the untimely death of his son. Killed by a dog at that, how undignified! Even in death his son was a disappointment to him. Carlyle had wanted to get cracking on the sequel, but his wife had convinced him otherwise, it would have just been in poor taste not to wait.

***

"Wanda! Where did you put that knitting needle?" Charlotte Douglas yelled. Wanda responded, "Don't fret, it's right beside the remote control." Charlotte's irritation left her as she was able to use the needle to relieve the itching under the cast, "Oh, thank you Wanda, you're a dear, I don't know how I would have managed to cope without your help. I'm so happy this cast is coming off tomorrow. But you will be staying on for a while yet won't you? I still won't be totally mobile for some time." Wanda assured her, "Of course I'll stay as long as you need me so don't worry about it, just concentrate on getting better."

Charlotte still felt rather annoyed with her carelessness. She hadn't been paying attention that day when she was going down the sweeping staircase. Well, it could have been worse, she could have fallen from the very top, not more towards the bottom. If that were the case she would have had more than one broken bone.

**

Even with the latest film on hold, Kato found she had a full schedule. All the magazines wanted her on their covers and she was constantly getting calls from reporters requesting interviews. So far she had managed to keep them at bay. She gave the excuse that she wasn't booking anything new until the new year.

It was nearing Thanksgiving and Kato was determined to have free time at Christmas. Toma was withdrawing more into himself and she felt like she really needed to be there for him.

**

Kato had gone to New York to do a personal appearance to help promote the line of cosmetics that she was the new face for. Now she was heading home and as the plane touched down she found herself impatient to get home.

Even before the taxi pulled up to the house, Kato could see a number of police cars. Her immediate thought was that they must have traced Brutus back to her! She asked the driver to drop her off at the front gates. She paid the fare and got out of the taxi on legs that were unsteady. She squared her shoulders and, walking tall, went forward to face her fate.

Chapter 15

The police officer approached her, "Are you Kato?" Kato said in a clear strong voice, "Yes I am." then braced herself. The officer continued, "I'm sorry miss, but there's been a terrible situation." Kato looked to where there was a group of officers. For the first time she noticed police tape marking off the area around the garage.

The officer took her arm, "Maybe we should go into the house." Once inside the officer sat Kato down before he continued. He explained that they had come to the house to talk with Toma and when they arrived they noticed the exhaust fumes and the sound of a running car coming from the garage. But when they had gotten there, it was too late, Toma had already passed away. Kato broke down in tears, "There must be some mistake!" The officer handed her a note that was in an evidence bag, "I'm sorry, but there's no mistake, he had it all planned out. This was next to him on the seat."

Kato took the bag and through the plastic and her tears read the note, *Kato, please forgive me but I must leave you. I know I should have confided in you that I had been diagnosed with cancer, but I didn't want you to try to convince me to go through treatment. I lived through Mika's pain and suffering as she fought for her life, and I didn't want to have to fight the same battle, with the possibility of the same results. Every day my pain has increased, not just the physical pain, but the pain in my heart. Don't be sad for me Kato, because I'll be with my Mika soon and forever. Again, please forgive me, and may God forgive me. Goodbye Kato. Love, Toma.*

Kato hung her head. The officer took the note from her trembling hands, and he went on to say, "The reason why we had wanted to speak with Mr. Kato is because of his dog. We've been investigating a fatal dog attack and had finally managed to track the dog by his ear tattoo. Kato's head was still bowed, so the officer didn't see the startled look on her face. The officer continued, "Mr. Kato was registered as the dog's owner, and we had come here to ask him some questions, but as it turns out, he had provided the answers in this other note he had written, addressed to the police. The officer held up the second note, also in an evidence bag. He didn't hand the note to her but just went on to say what was in it, "In this note he states that on the night of Fraser Douglas' death he had forgotten to close the gate that usually keeps the dog confined. He also mentioned about the dog's medical condition, something that the vet had collaborated earlier. The vet blames himself for not having put the dog down at the time of diagnosis."

Kato had thought earlier that nothing could make her feel worse than she already did but she had been wrong. Even when Toma was at his lowest low he had still thought about Kato and protected her. She couldn't stop the flow of tears. The officer asked, "Is there anyone you would like us to call?" She thought for a moment.

Karen.   She asked the officer to contact Karen
Tillerman.

***

Karen was at work when the police tracked her down.
She made arrangements right away to leave work and
be with her friend. She had let her friend down once
before and she owed it to Kato to be there for her this
time. Karen got there just before the onslaught of
reporters. The few remaining police officers on the
scene acted fast and held them at bay, keeping the
situation under control.

Kato and Karen watched it all from the safety of the
house. Karen thought, what kind of animals were these
people? Hadn't this poor woman been through enough?
Yet here they were, circling like vultures.

Karen wasn't sure that this was the right time to give it
to Kato, but at least it would be a bit of good news, and
she had promised Vera that she would deliver it to Kato
in person. Karen handed Kato the pale blue envelope.
Kato opened it and looked at the elaborate wedding
invitation announcing the union of Vera and Antonio.
Vera and Tony had set the wedding date and Kato was
happy for them, although her happiness was fleeting as
the reality of this horrible day came back to her.
However, the wedding would be something to look
forward to, a reason to go on. She would mark the day
on her calendar.

***

The next week was like a circus. They had to arrange for an entourage of security guards to keep the press and public away from the house. The funeral had been a nightmare, with constant distractions whenever someone tried to break through the security line and a struggle would ensue.

***

It was finally over, but Kato almost preferred the chaos, at least then she hadn't been left alone with her own thoughts, thoughts that haunted and tormented her. Why? Why had he done it? And why hadn't she seen it coming? Or had she? She had noticed that Toma had been withdrawing into himself. Why hadn't she stepped in, insisted on getting to the bottom of what was bothering him? Toma had played such an important part in her life, she owed everything to him yet when he had needed her, she hadn't been there for him. She didn't know if she could ever forgive herself.

***

There was a round of applause as Viktor stood for the first time. But his victory was short-lived, almost immediately he felt his legs give way under him. He still had a long way to go. His physiotherapy was done for the day and it was time for him to be taken home. Home, one could hardly call his empty house a home. Without Kato to share it, every part of his life felt empty. He had heard about Toma's suicide. It tore him up inside when he thought of what Kato was probably going through right now.

Since being a hit and run victim Viktor had a lot of time to think about Kato, about the pain that she would have gone through after being attacked, and *that* had been a deliberate act! He now understood why Kato had reacted the way she did when her attacker came back into her life. He thought of how angry and bitter he felt towards the driver that had hit him and left him for dead, and that wasn't even a deliberate act! If they ever found the person, would he leave it up to the courts to get justice, or would he take the law into his own hands? Although Viktor wanted to reach out to Kato he couldn't contact her, not now. He didn't want her to see him like this.

Viktor's thoughts turned to Toma's suicide and he couldn't help but feel a pang of guilt. Could he have prevented it? Maybe if he had seen through Toma's lame story of wanting to retire, maybe then things would have turned out differently. He became more and more frustrated thinking of "what ifs" and "maybes". To distract himself from his thoughts he buried himself in his work.

***

Christmas and New Year's Eve both went by unobserved by Kato. She looked at the new calendar she had just put up and hoped that this year was going to be better than the last one. She then looked at the clock on the wall and decided it was best that she get to bed as she had to be at the lawyer's the next day for the reading of Toma's will. The reading had been delayed because they were waiting for Mrs. White, the cook to return from her vacation. She had been out of town visiting her daughter over the Christmas holidays.

***

Kato sat with Mrs. White and Ms. Easton in the lawyer's office, waiting for the reading of Toma's will. There were no relatives present. Toma's parents had passed away years ago and he had never been in touch or gotten to know any relatives in Japan. And of course, he didn't have any children. Wanda Stock was to be there too but was running a bit late. Once she arrived the reading began.

Toma had left generous sums to all three of the women who had worked for him, but the bulk went to Kato. His business, his properties, the house, they now all belonged to her. After the will was read and they were all leaving, the lawyer asked Kato to stay behind, there were a few more things he wanted to go over with her.

The lawyer went into the details of the proposal Toma had put to another corporation. She was surprised by this news as she had no idea Toma had been planning on selling the company, but then again, it must have all been part of his larger plan. Kato bit her lip to stop it from quivering. The lawyer continued, "I'm not suggesting that you should or shouldn't continue with the sale, but it's something you should think about. If you want, I could represent you in the matter, or if you would feel more comfortable with your own lawyer, please feel free to go through him. Here is my card and I'll also give you the name and number of the man Toma was negotiating with." Kato looked at the name he had written down on the back of his business card, *Viktor Cross*.

***

That night Kato had a lot to consider. She was in a dilemma. She knew nothing about running the real estate business, and yet, she couldn't hire someone to run it, not with the possibility of it being sold. If the sale went through, that person could be out the door, it wouldn't be fair to them. On the other hand, without proper supervision, the business could slide, and she couldn't allow that to happen, Toma had dedicated too much of his life building it up to where it was now. She would have to come to a decision soon.

***

Rumours could be heard throughout the real estate office. Everyone was on edge, everyone that is that had ever snubbed, insulted or given Kato a hard time. How were they to know that one day their bullying would backfire on them. Kato was now the one who held their fate in her hands. They were all waiting, wondering what would happen next.

***

Wanda Stock drove up to the Douglas house. Charlotte Douglas had been very understanding about Wanda's grief, but of course she would be, she had suffered a great loss not that long ago. Mrs. Douglas no longer needed her services, but she just wanted to drop by and make sure she was doing okay emotionally. A servant let her in and announced her presence. As Wanda entered the living room, she noticed Charlotte put a framed photo back on an end table. Wanda noticed it was a photo of Charlotte's son and she said, "A tragedy, what happened to your son, I'm so sorry for your loss."

Charlotte nodded her head in acknowledgment and replied, "Thank you, and I'm very sorry for your loss as well. Please, sit, and tell me, how was it that you came to know Mr. Kato?" Wanda sat down and began, "I was hired by him to look after his wife when she was being treated for cancer and then again to look after a young woman who had come into his care a few years back. She had been a victim of a vicious attack, almost didn't make it, but Mr. Kato took her in, covered the costs of all of her surgeries. She went on to great things, became a model and an actor." Wanda continued, "Poor Toma, he had felt so bad having made her into the image of his deceased wife, but she didn't seem to mind, in fact, she embraced her new image, even colouring her red hair black and wearing brown contacts to cover her green eyes."

While Wanda had rambled on, Charlotte had listened intently, and once Wanda had stopped talking, she asked, "This woman, did she happen to have a dog?" Wanda thought for a moment, "Yes, it was just a pup back then, but it grew into a monstrous thing, although it was friendly enough." Wanda noticed that Charlotte had paled, and assumed that she had tired, so Wanda took her leave.

After Wanda had left Charlotte started putting the pieces of the puzzle together. So, she was alive! Cassandra Carrington was alive and well and living her life as Kato. She had even been in their home. She was just digesting all of this when the doorbell rang. Now who? She asked herself. The servant came into the room and announced that the police would like to speak with her.

The police didn't stay long, they had just wanted her to know that they had found the owner of the dog that had attacked her son. After the officers left, Charlotte had even more puzzle pieces to put together. She didn't quite believe the information the police had given her about the dog being on the loose because of an open gate. She didn't have any proof, but she believed that Cassandra Carrington was responsible for her son's death.

Charlotte heard the front door open, and Carlyle stormed in, "I'll sue the bastard's estate!" Carlyle had just come from his office where the police had given him the same information that Charlotte had just gotten. Charlotte had to think fast, a lawsuit was the last thing that they wanted to start, it might bring out the whole ugly truth about Fraser. She managed to calm Carlyle down and eventually convince him that it would be bad publicity to sue, after all, it wasn't like they needed the money. Carlyle grumbled but agreed.

***

What could Kato say but "yes" to Charlotte Douglas' invitation, although it seemed to Kato to be more of a summons. She rang the doorbell and was surprised when Charlotte herself opened the door, "Please come in Kato, or should I call you Cassandra?" So she knew! Kato fought to keep her composure and replied, "I've become quite accustomed to Kato, thank you."

Charlotte, walking with the use of a cane, led Kato into the study. Charlotte motioned to a chair, "Please, sit." Kato sat and watched the other woman as she started mixing a couple of drinks, "I know the invitation was to tea, but after what I have to say, you're probably going to need one of these." Charlotte handed her one of the drinks then sat in the chair opposite Kato. Kato was totally unprepared for what was to come.

Charlotte started, "First, I want you to know that my husband and I won't be launching a lawsuit against Mr. Kato's estate. I also want to make it quite clear to you that I know the role you played in my son's death." Wow! Kato thought, that was laying it on the line! Charlotte continued, "But I don't have any proof, and I have my own reasons for not going to the police, but that's not why I asked you here." The second statement was more shocking to Kato than the first had been. Charlotte went on, "I'd better start from the beginning. My husband, Carlyle, is your biological father." Kato put her hand to her mouth in horror! *He*, Carlyle Douglas was her father! That would mean Fraser would have been her half-brother! She could feel herself becoming physically ill.

Charlotte watched Kato's reaction and couldn't help but feel some satisfaction, but she went on to say, "I'd better explain something, Carlyle wasn't Fraser's biological father." Kato's nausea started to subside, and she waited for Charlotte to continue. Charlotte explained, "While Carlyle was off having his affairs, I was having a few of my own. Of course, he never suspected. It never occurred to him that I would be less than satisfied with the few crumbs of affection he threw my way. So, when I got pregnant, of course, he thought Fraser was his, why would he think otherwise? It helped that Fraser had my looks, which was fortunate as Fraser's

218

biological father had red hair." Kato was wondering what Charlotte was getting to, and she was about to find out as the other woman continued, "Then your mother came along, and she became pregnant with you. She must have threatened to come to me with the truth because he had set her up in one of his houses, something he had never done with any of his other mistresses. I knew all along, but let him think I was clueless. I got years of enjoyment watching him squirm and hide the situation from me."

Charlotte stopped for a moment when she saw Kato's expression. Charlotte went on, "I know what's running through your head right now, but don't think that you became an actor only because of Carlyle pulling some strings for your mother. He just happened to luck out that your talent was real."

Kato was surprised by the compliment and listened intently as Charlotte continued, "Now, to get on to when you and Fraser met. Carlyle was furious and dead set against it, thinking of course that you and Fraser were half-sister and brother. Of course I knew otherwise and took great pleasure in watching my husband squirm. Unfortunately, my not speaking up caused all of us a lot of grief. If I had come clean, you and Fraser could have been together, maybe had a life together, but because of the circumstances, your relationship had disastrous results."

Kato spoke up, "But why are you telling me all of this now?" Charlotte looked directly into her eyes, "I was just coming to that, and I hope you're ready for this. I believe that your mother's car accident was no accident, that Carlyle arranged it. I believe that he murdered your mother."

The shock was too much and Kato started to black out. She heard Charlotte say, "Here, drink this." It was the potent mixture that had been handed to her earlier. She took a large gulp and coughed as the liquid burned her throat. Charlotte waited for the coughing to stop then continued, "The night of your mother's accident, she came here to meet Carlyle. He had her ushered into the study, but then made her wait for half an hour. He had gone out of the house during that time and when he came back inside, he went upstairs to change his shirt. It wasn't until after your mother left that I noticed the shirt in the hamper, and it had brake fluid on it. I was going to take the shirt to the police the next day, but couldn't find it anywhere. The proof was gone and it would have been his word against mine."

Kato was becoming faint again. She took another drink of the concoction in her glass and then asked, "But why are you telling me all of this now?" Charlotte explained, "I would have told you sooner, but I thought you were dead. But now, our lives are again intertwined and I felt I should warn you what you're up against, Carlyle is a dangerous man. I'm hoping that you might remember something from that night or around the time of your mother's death that could incriminate him. So if you think of anything, please let me know. If I could put him behind bars, I would." With that final statement the visit was over.

***

Charlotte watched as Kato drove through the open gates of the estate. She thought that Kato must have wondered why, if Charlotte knew about her role in Fraser's death, she hadn't turned her in to the police. It was Charlotte's pride that wouldn't let her do it. She would rather the world think of her son as an innocent victim rather than the animal that he had turned out to be. How then, would she be judged by everyone as to what kind of mother could bring up such a monster? She also thought that aside from maybe being able to help her put Carlyle behind bars. If she had the choice of Kato going to jail or Carlyle, she would choose Carlyle, that's how much she despised him.

***

Kato's head was still spinning when she got home. Her biggest shock of the night was that although Charlotte knew about her role in Fraser's death, she hadn't informed the police. Close behind was the shock that Carlyle had killed her mother, that Carlyle and her mother had been lovers, that her mother had resorted to blackmail, and that Carlyle was her father!

Kato went to her bedroom and sat at the vanity, and stared at herself in the mirror. She thought of how, through fate, her face had become the face of a stranger. *That* she was able to live with, what she wasn't sure she could live with was that when she looked at her reflection and into her eyes, all she could see was the ugly soul of Carlyle Douglas. He was a part of her DNA; he was a part of *her*!

The life she had lived had been one big lie! She got up and began pacing; she didn't know what to do with herself. She dragged out the cardboard box that held all of the sympathy cards she had received after her mother's death. Where was the one from Carlyle Douglas? She was going to destroy it! It was just one more lie! To think she had been so touched when it had arrived. But his sympathetic gesture had been a big farce! She found the card, placed back in its envelope like all of the others. She held it with both hands and was about to rip it in half when she looked at the postmark, really looked at it for the first time. The postmark date was July 15th. Her mother's accident was on the evening of July 15th. He had already signed and mailed out the sympathy card *before* her mother's death. No wonder she had received it so quickly. She stared again at the envelope. Carlyle Douglas had murdered her mother, and she had always had the proof right under her nose!

Her hands were trembling so much that she had to use both hands to carry the envelope over to her nightstand. She was ever so careful with it, almost as it if were capable of breaking. She was suddenly very exhausted. She slipped between the sheets in hopes of getting a good night's sleep. She was going to need all of her energy to set her plan into motion, and the sooner she did, the better. She couldn't wait for justice to be done, but first she had to get organized. She just hoped that Charlotte Douglas had meant it when she said that she wanted her husband behind bars. When the time was right, it was going to take the two of them to bring him down.

Chapter 16

Viktor hung up the phone. He had wondered what Kato's decision was going to be and now he knew, she was going to sell. He had to admit that it hurt though, having been contacted by her lawyer. She couldn't even stand to talk to him in person. Well, if that was the way things were going to be, then so be it. He would have his own lawyer give her a call in the morning, it was probably best that way anyhow, keep it all business.

*****

Well, it was about time! Carlyle had been chomping at the bit to get going on the sequel to "Dragon of Danger" and now everything was a go. It had been a long time coming, though, with negotiations dragging on with the lead female actor. He had found her demands to be rather odd; she hadn't wanted more money, in fact, she didn't want any at all. What she did want was some stock he owned. He had been reluctant to give it up but, in the end, gave in. She had also demanded to have her own private trailer and, of all things, insisted on being able to do her own hair and makeup. But he still figured he had come out ahead in the deal, she was good and was going to make a lot of money for him. In fact, in the sequel, "Midnight Mission of Angels" he had the writers rewrite the script to focus more on Kato's role.

***

Everyone wanted this hot commodity. They all wanted her face on the covers of their magazines and her body in their clothes. The calls kept coming in, but Kato had the same answer for every one of them, she wasn't doing any more modeling at this time. She had other agendas. The phone rang yet again. Ah! This was a call she had been waiting for, she asked, "How did you make out?... Almost all of it?... Great! The next time you call I want it to be to let me know that you got it all." Kato hung up and felt in control for the first time in her life. She knew what she wanted, and she was feeling close to getting it.

***

It was time for Kato to call in a favour. She took the business card and called the cell phone number scrawled on the back of it. The person at the other end of the line was surprised to hear from her but was more than happy to oblige her. After the call ended Kato let out a sigh of relief. Well, that was fairly painless. Max the Machine had agreed to be her date for Vera's wedding. She went to her closet and looked for something to wear to the big event. She thought of the unspoken wedding rules, okay, nothing white, black or red. Hmm. After dismissing dress after dress, she decided on a body-skimming, low-cut beige dress, covered entirely in clear sequins. It was to be quite the splashy affair and the dress had some pizazz but wouldn't outshine the bride. Nude pumps and the star necklace that Toma had given her would complete the outfit.

***

The bride was radiant. Vera's pale blonde hair was set in Veronica Lake waves. Her slim classically cut dress, covered in crystal beads, added to the look of old-Hollywood glamour. At first, Kato had thought Valentine's Day an odd day for a wedding, but in retrospect thought that at least it should guarantee that Vera's husband never forgot their anniversary date. It was a grand affair, held in a swanky hotel that was costing an arm and a leg. When Kato had received the wedding invitation and saw where it was being held, she had offered, as her wedding gift to them, to pay for the room rental and reception, going so far as to make all of the arrangements. It would be one less thing for the couple to have to worry about.

Someone looks way too serious, come on!" said Karen as she grabbed Kato's arm and started pulling her into a crowd of women in the middle of the room. Kato started to pull away once she realized Karen's intentions, but then Jen came to help Karen in her quest. Many of the women in the crowd had determined looks on their faces; they meant business. It was every woman for herself. The mob got uglier, moving forward until they were pressed together like cattle. The bride was ready to throw the bouquet.

Karen and Jen both got caught up in the moment and Kato took the opportunity to make her way to the back of the crowd. She had just broken free from the group when from the corner of her eye she saw something coming at her. She instinctively raised her arm, not realizing what had happened until it was too late, she had caught the bouquet!

"Some people have all the luck!" wailed Jen. Barbara piped in, "Well if you ask me, I'd consider it to be bad luck!" Karen teased, "Oh ya? I noticed you were up there with the rest of us." While the two women were bantering Kato left to find Max and together they said their goodbyes and best wishes to the bride and groom. Vera squealed, "So you're the one who caught the bouquet." and turned her attention to Max, "So do I hear wedding bells in your future?" Kato laughed, "Come on Max, we'd better get out of here fast, the minister is still here, and we don't want her getting any ideas."

Although Max had escorted Kato to the wedding, he was just a friend. They were still laughing about Vera's comments as they walked through the doors of the banquet room so they were caught off guard by the reporters and photographers waiting in the lobby of the hotel.

"Can we get a comment from the happy couple?" one reporter shouted. After their initial surprise, Max and Kato smirked at each other and then, without saying a word, embraced in a long hard kiss. Still without a word, they left hand in hand, making a mad dash to the limousine. The press was following and gaining on them. Kato hit on an idea. Pausing for just a moment, she threw the bouquet behind her. Flashbulbs went off and created enough of a diversion for them to make their getaway.

Kato couldn't believe it, how did they know where she was? Then it hit her, "Oh my God! They must have gotten wind that I had booked the room! And wouldn't you know it, I just happened to have the bouquet as we came out!" Max was thoughtful, "Hmm, now I know the woman who catches the bouquet is supposed to be the next one to get married, but what happens if that person throws the bouquet too? Does it mean they throw away their chance of ever getting married?" Kato gave him a playful pinch on his cheek, "Well, in that case, you'll just have to be my escort, *forever*!" "Oh no! Stop! You're scaring me!" teased Max.

Once their playful bantering was over, Kato's mood turned serious. She thought about Max's earlier comment about throwing her chance away. As far ash she was concerned, she already had.

***

Veronica Sutton studied her face in the mirror and was quite satisfied with the results. She figured her new nose was going to be a good investment. It had already proved beneficial. During her stay at the hospital she had run across Viktor Cross, Kato's former lover.

It took some convincing, and a few bribes, but Veronica had finally been able to get some information about Viktor from his physiotherapist. She knew his likes, his dislikes, even that he had a birthmark that resembled a butterfly on his butt. She had made a point of befriending him, hoping that, in time, he would confide in her about Kato. Veronica just knew that there had to be something there that she could use against the other woman, she just had to get closer to him.

Veronica thought Viktor might be of assistance to her in another area too, after all, he was a very attractive man, and now that he was completely recovered from his accident, she was determined to take advantage of his renewed strength.

***

Viktor was feeling his old self, the purchase of Toma's business, well, actually Kato's business, had been finalized, and now he was ready to get on with his life. He rolled over on his side and reached over to the nightstand. He held the ring in his hand, turning it this way and that, watching the way it would shine when the light hit it at a certain angle. Brilliant green, like the green of her eyes.

Viktor was feeling optimistic when he got up that morning. He headed to the kitchen where he knew his automatic coffee maker would have a steaming cup of brew ready for him. He grabbed the cup, at the same time grabbing his cell phone as it rang. It was his sister Susan, and she got right to the point. What she said caused him to drop his cup. It shattered, sending ceramic shards and hot coffee everywhere. "Damn! I've got to go; I'll talk to you later."

Viktor left the mess as it was, it could wait. First he had to check out Susan's story, she had to be mistaken. He logged onto his computer and checked out various news sites, all of which carried the same story. So it was true!

The mess in the kitchen remained as it had been. Viktor, so full of hope earlier, now just wanted to collapse. He sank heavily into an armchair and stared straight ahead. How could she? Married and to that big gorilla! The only thing that had motivated him to get well, to walk again, was the thought of being able to walk up to Kato and take her in his arms, but now...!

Viktor closed his eyes. The images in the photographs haunted him, her in the beige sequined dress, the bouquet of pale pink roses, the shot as she threw it into the air, and that kiss! Viktor felt like his world was coming crashing down around him.

***

The cast and crew all knew she wasn't really married, but they razzed her about it anyhow. Kato really didn't mind; it was all in good fun. She just hoped that the extra publicity didn't throw too much notice her way right now. She still had to get the word out to the press that it was all a sham, but for now, she wanted to lay low.

It was time for Kato to get to work. She had thrown herself into the role. She had studied martial arts and kickboxing, not just for the role but also for her own personal protection. She never again wanted to be in such a vulnerable position as she had been on the beach that day she had been attacked. All of her hard work had paid off, she looked lean and mean for the camera. The role was physically draining, and she was all but done in when she heard the director yell, "Okay, take five!"

Kato rushed to her trailer. They had been shooting a scene outside, and she had been sweltering in the hot sun. The wig certainly didn't help, but for now, it was a necessary evil. She pulled if off of her head and shook out her long hair. Ever since shooting for the movie began, she had stopped colouring her hair black, and now as her hair grew, her own natural copper colour was taking over.

Even though she was sweltering, a shiver ran down her spine. How she hated that man! Carlyle had decided to be present on the set today, and it took all she had not to strangle him with her bare hands. She was becoming more and more agitated. She had to calm down. She took some long, deep breaths then quickly drank some bottled water then touched up her makeup. This next part she dreaded, she wound her hair up and pinned it to the top of her head, then put on the hot, sweaty wig. It was time to go back out there.

The action started again, and Kato gave it her all. She was determined that the shooting would finish as scheduled. She had no control over the editing process, but she was keeping her fingers crossed. She needed the movie to hit the theatres in time to be considered at the next Academy Awards. She hadn't really cared about missing out on an Oscar for "Dragon of Danger", but, this time, around she *had* to get an Oscar. So much was riding on it.

***

Viktor couldn't believe he had agreed to this date. He had been evasive, always having an excuse not to get together, but he had run out of excuses, and Veronica Sutton wasn't taking "no" for an answer. As he got ready to go, he felt uneasy, somehow he couldn't shake the feeling that Veronica had a hidden agenda.

***

Kato had been going non-stop during the filming, but with that now over and her not having accepted any modeling jobs, she was at a loose end. When Max called up and asked her to dinner, she was ready for the distraction and accepted. As Kato was getting ready for the dinner date, she couldn't help but wonder about Max's invitation. They usually only got together when she needed an escort to special functions. Something was up.

***

Max couldn't remember the last time he was so nervous. He opened the small velvet box and took out the diamond ring. The diamond shone like so many pinpoints of light. Max studied the large two carat stone. It seemed almost too large for the gold band that it adorned. He looked through the center of the band. It looked so tiny, but then it would have to be, to fit her very slim finger. It was time for him to go. He put the ring back into the box and snapped the lid shut.

***

Max pulled out Kato's chair, and she couldn't help but smile. She thought back to when they had first met and how he had been such a jerk. Fortunately, he had seen the error of his ways and had turned out to be a pretty decent guy. She couldn't help but feel that she had played a role in the new improved Max.

As they ate their meal, Kato noticed Max was preoccupied, and nervous. This was something new, Max, nervous? She was about to comment on it when Max blurted out, "Kato, there's something I've got to talk to you about." She wasn't sure if she was going to like this or not, but she let Max speak.

Married! Somehow Kato had never thought of Max getting married, and to Jen at that! She didn't even know they had been seeing one another. Max explained that they had been secretly seeing each other ever since they had met at Vera's wedding. Jen didn't want to say anything to her because she wasn't sure how Kato would feel about it. Max and Jen, she couldn't think of a more mismatched couple physically, but she could see how Max, close to seven feet tall and muscle-bound, who really was just a big teddy bear, would feel very protective towards Jen, a petite little thing that barely weighed ninety pounds. And Jen was the kind of woman that yearned for that protection and security, so on second thought, she couldn't think of a better match.

Kato was overjoyed, "That's great news when's the big day?" Max confessed that he hadn't asked her yet, that she probably wouldn't say yes unless she knew that Kato was okay with it. Kato was ecstatic and said, "Well you tell her I'm more than okay with it, and I insist that she say yes! This calls for a celebration!" She motioned the waiter to come over, and she ordered champagne and said to Max, "Tonight is on me!" The waiter brought the bubbly right away and after their glasses were filled Kato raised her glass, "Here's to the future!" "To the future!" echoed Max. Their glasses clinked, and Kato almost dropped hers as she saw Viktor walk through the door with Veronica Sutton.

Viktor noticed her the moment he walked through the door. Of all the people he had to run into tonight it had to be her. Maybe it was for the best he thought, after all, she had obviously moved on with her life, so why not let her think that he had moved on with his? He made a point of being attentive to Veronica, listening to her banter, laughing at her witty comments. He had managed to convince her that he was having a good time, now if only he could convince himself. He had to admit that he was relieved when Veronica excused herself to go to the ladies room.

Veronica had noticed Kato get up from her table, and head to the washroom and Veronica decided to do the same. While Veronica waited for Kato to come out of the stall, she made a pretense of fixing her flawless makeup. Even though Viktor had tried to hide it, Veronica could see that he still had feelings for Kato, but she was determined to make sure that Kato thought otherwise. She knew exactly what she was going to say.

As Kato came up to the sink, Veronica gushed, "I noticed you're drinking champagne tonight, you must be celebrating something big. So are me and Viktor. Of course every day is a celebration when we're together, he's just so irresistible, especially his cute butt, and that butterfly-shaped birthmark is so adorable! Well, have a fun evening!"

Kato watched Veronica breeze out of the room. She decided to touch up her makeup, not that a touch up was necessary, but she needed a few moments to compose herself. Veronica had made it quite clear that she and Viktor were an item. And they must be, otherwise, how would Veronica have known about the birthmark?

***

With Veronica away from the table, Viktor had taken the opportunity to steal another glance at Kato's table. He was disappointed to see that she was gone. Just the large man with the big stupid grin on his face was there. Viktor remembered a time when the man with the big grin on his face used to be him.

Veronica came back to the table, and Viktor suggested that they leave. Veronica took his suggestion as an invitation to continue the date at her place, and he didn't argue, he just wanted to get out of there before Kato returned to her table. He didn't think he could bear to see the happy couple together.

***

Kato finally returned to her table. She apologized to Max for taking so long. Giving the age old excuse of a headache, she asked that they call it a night. The ride home was spent in silence, but a comfortable one. Max, being the gentleman he had become, escorted her to the door. As much as her heart was breaking, she was genuinely happy for Max and Jen, and she gave him a big hug, "Goodnight Max, and good luck with Jen, I wish you both all the best." She watched him leave, almost skipping back to the taxi. She couldn't help but envy his happiness. She thought of how Max had talked about Jen. He was so smitten with her. Kato had to smile to herself when she thought about petite Jen and how she was probably going to be able to wrap that giant of a man around her little finger.

***

Viktor had to wonder what he was even doing at Veronica's place; he wasn't interested in her at all. Normally in such circumstances, he would have already excused himself, but he was feeling vulnerable tonight and lonely. It didn't take long for her to make moves on him, and he found himself kissing her back.

Viktor felt like he was a pinball machine. It was like Veronica was trying to hit all of his erogenous zones, as if the more she touched on, the more points she was going to get. Didn't she realize how mechanical her love-making was? How it lacked passion? Passion, now Kato had passion. He thought of Kato now, how when she had touched his skin, it was because she had wanted to feel it, feel him! She was guided by her emotions, not like this conniving woman who was pawing at him right now. It was no good; this just wasn't working for him. He took Veronica's hands and removed them from his body. He made a lame excuse about having a lot to do the next day, then took his leave. Damn! Thought Veronica as she slammed the door after he left. She went to her bedroom and opened the top drawer of her dresser and grabbed her stash of drugs.

***

It turned out that Viktor did have a busy day ahead of him. He had been undecided as to what to do with the staff at his new real estate business. Ordinarily, if things were running smoothly he would let things go on as they were, but that wasn't the situation in this case. When Kato had confided in him about who she really was, she had also mentioned about the time she worked for Toma, and how the other workers had tried to make her life miserable. He couldn't keep employees that he couldn't trust so he had decided to do a restructuring of both his existing real estate business and the new one, giving him justification to transfer some of his own staff over to the new business, and laying off the staff from the newly acquired office. When he had bought the business from Kato, there wasn't anything in the agreement stating that their jobs were to be guaranteed. Kato had deliberately left that wide open so that his hands would not be tied to keeping them on, so the decision was his to make. Viktor was trying to convince himself that what he was doing was for the good of the company, not because he was getting revenge on the people who had treated Kato so callously.

Chapter 17

The phone rang, "Derrick Wade here... oh, hi Veronica... no luck? Well listen, I know we had agreed that between the two of us we were going to dig up the dirt on Kato, but right now there are bigger things going on right here at work, gotta go." Derrick wrinkled his brow. He was used to victimizing people, but today the shoe could be on the other foot. Rumours had been flying around the office that "The Limelight" had been bought by a sole owner and that there were going to be big changes.

The word was out, and the whole office was in a panic. The new owner had called a meeting and would be stopping by that morning to make an announcement. The meeting was set for ten o'clock, and it was now five minutes to ten. Silence fell as they waited for the new owner to walk through the door. At one minute to, the door opened. All heads turned as Kato walked into the building.

What she said shocked everyone. "The Limelight" as they knew it, was no longer going to exist. There would be no more printed word. She was taking "The Limelight" and turning it into a hour-long television entertainment program. It would continue to feature celebrities and cover the same events it always had, but now it would be done with integrity and truth. The days of sensationalism were gone. And gone would be those that didn't have the training and knowledge needed to work in the electronic medium. Photographers would be replaced with people with video camera experience; in-your-face reporters would be replaced by well-known and popular celebrity hosts.

Those being let go would receive a month's severance pay, but as of today, they would no longer be working for "The Limelight." All the time that Kato had been speaking, there had been a couple of people that Kato had brought to the office with her. While she had been talking, they had been handing out pink slips to various employees. Once the slips were all handed out, Kato continued, "Those of you who have received your notice, please pack up your personal belongings. You are to leave your computers as they are; they will be shut down later." Kato also announced that the company would be offering a workshop on resume writing and job searching the following week for any of the departing employees who wanted to attend.

After Kato had left, there was total silence as each of those employees given notice started to clean out their respective desks. There was nothing left to be said; they had obviously pissed off the wrong person.

***

It took months of hard work and a lot of money, but "The Limelight" was finally fully revamped, and the first program was set to air the week before Christmas.

The network that had picked it up had initially had its doubts when Kato had approached them, what with "The Limelight's" past reputation, but had finally been convinced to take it on board. Kato was going to make sure that they didn't regret it.

***

The network had been promoting the show a whole month before it was to start airing, causing a lot of hype. Now that the big day had arrived, they expected record numbers to be watching.

***

Viktor wasn't immune to all of the hype. He found himself sitting in front of his television waiting for the show to start. He was impressed by the way it had been put together, the dynamic set, the professionalism, and charisma of the hosts. But then, he would expect nothing less from the woman behind it all. The show was informative, reporting on upcoming events and movies, including "Midnight Mission of Angels" that had opened at the box office that week. It was already breaking box office records and was rumoured to be an Academy Award winner in the spring. Viktor had to admit that the show was also entertaining, featuring interviews with various celebrities. There was one interview in particular that caught his attention; it was Max the Machine talking about his recent engagement. He listened intently as Max dispelled the rumours about his marriage to Kato, and how it was that circumstances made it appear that they had gotten married. Suddenly Viktor was in the Christmas spirit!

The show came to an end, and the crew let out hoots and hollers. They could tell by the way it had gone today that the show was going to be a success. Kato gave a sigh of relief. She had really invested a lot in this project, both financially and emotionally, and now it was turning out to be a winner. She was about to join the celebrations when she was pulled aside. There was someone wishing to see her.

She went to the front to see who it was and was greeted by a bright bouquet of flowers. She took hold of the flowers and lowered them so that she could see the person behind them, "Cole!" He was the last person she had expected to see, "What are you doing here in America?" she asked in surprise.

Cole explained that he came to amalgamate his wine company with one in California. His ex-wife had the kids for Christmas this year, so he was at a loose end. Kato wasn't sure how she felt about being a stand-in, but what the heck, she was at a loose end herself this holiday season, so he would do in a pinch, "Have you any plans for New Year's Eve?" she asked.

***

No! Susan had to be joking! Take his sister out for New Years Eve! Susan was hell-bent on convincing him, "Come on Viktor, I even have a sitter lined up for the night, do you realize how hard it is to swing that for New Year's Eve?" Viktor groaned, "What was it you said happened with Rod?" Susan explained, "He got called away out of town on business, and I don't want these tickets, or my sitter, to go to waste." Viktor grumbled, "Okay, but just don't expect me to enjoy it." "You're the best!" Susan replied and hung up before he could change his mind.

***

Kato thought about her date for the night. She had her doubts about Cole. She thought back to when she was in Italy, how he hadn't stood up to his mother, even when she had been so openly insulting to his guest. It wasn't that she had anything against him, but could she ever be serious about anyone so spineless? He had also made it clear, perhaps not intentionally, that she wasn't his first choice of companion for the holidays. She thought of Vera's words, how a woman wants a man to make her feel special. No, Cole definitely did not make her feel special.

Thinking of Cole made her think of Italy, and shoes. She still hadn't worn the gold-tone sandals she had bought there. She would wear them tonight, with the dress she had bought them to wear with. She took the gown out of the closet; it really was cleverly designed, the peacock's body following the line of the dress, which in turn, showed off every curve of her body. Dangling gold earrings added the finishing touch. She noticed a section of hair that had fallen down from the up-swept style. She felt the texture of it as she pinned it back into place. It wasn't as silky-soft as her own hair but, as far as wigs went, it was as close as it could get to the real thing. She had been having her own hair trimmed periodically, and the black was now totally gone, but the time was not yet right to reveal her own copper tresses.

***

"Ah, so that's the infamous dress," noted Barbara as Kato and Cole joined their small group. Jen and Max were there, along with Vera and Tony. Karen and Barbara had both gone stag. Once Kato made the introductions, Cole excused himself to get a couple of drinks.

***

Viktor caught sight of Kato right away. It was hard to miss her in that dress. His heart skipped a beat, and he almost headed in her direction, but then he saw the hand, casually touching her back. It belonged to a man who was looking admiring down at Kato.

Susan had noticed something, or someone had caught her brother's eye. She looked over to where he had been looking and saw her, Kato. Looking at her brother now, one wouldn't know he was upset, but having known him all her life, Susan knew he was hurting.

***

Karen was making weird signals. It took Kato awhile to catch on that Karen was trying to let her know that she should turn around. Kato turned, and it didn't take her long to pick Viktor out in the crowd. She had expected to see Veronica by his side, but instead saw his sister Susan. She found it rather odd but had to admit that she was relieved that he wasn't with Veronica.

***

It was almost midnight. Cole was busy talking with Barbara and Kato took the opportunity to slip away to the ladies room. She had noticed throughout the evening Cole's roving eyes, ogling almost every woman that came into his line of vision. It wasn't that she was jealous, but she simply found his actions to be a turn-off. Come midnight, she had no wish to be kissing Cole.

She was standing in front of the washroom mirror when Susan came out of one of the stalls. Although Kato's relationship with Viktor hadn't worked out, the two women had gotten along on the few occasions that they had been in each others company, and they genuinely wished each other a happy new year. Susan hesitated, then said, "I'm really sorry that it didn't work out between you and Viktor. He never told me what your tiff was about, but I almost feel that if he hadn't had his accident when he did..." Kato cut in, "Accident?" Susan looked at Kato in surprise, "You mean you never knew? He never told you?" Kato shook her head. Susan pulled Kato over to the side where there was a small padded bench and relayed the whole sad story about the hit and run accident.

By the time they had finished talking it was well past midnight. Everyone would wonder where she had gotten to. She excused herself and headed back to her group. Making her apologies.

***

Viktor had watched for Kato at midnight, but he hadn't seen her since she had gone into the washroom, the same place that Susan had gone shortly before her. He then noticed that they both came out of the washroom at the same time. His eyes weren't on Susan when she came back to where he stood; they were on Kato. He couldn't help but notice that Kato and her date didn't kiss once she rejoined him. Good! Viktor thought to himself.

***

The evening ended on a rather flat note for Kato. Cole had been somewhat put out by Kato's absence at midnight and was sulking. Kato had no patience for Cole's sulky mood and just wanted the night to end. They parted on rather cool terms. It wasn't a very exciting beginning to the new year, but Kato had a glimmer of hope because it appeared to her that Viktor didn't have anyone in his life at the moment. Kato crossed her fingers.

***

Once in bed, Kato thought back to her conversation with Susan. So Viktor had been critically hurt. She thought about how he must have suffered physically and mentally, not knowing if he would ever walk again. It must have happened shortly after their last meeting when he had come to see her to find out if she had anything to do with Fraser's death. She had to wonder if the accident had been part of the reason she hadn't heard from him, or was it just because he despised her so much?

***

The Academy Awards were fast approaching and, as predicted, Kato was nominated for the Best Female Actor award for her leading role in "Midnight Mission of Angels." She picked up a framed photograph of her mother. She had to win this year; she just *had* to. "This will be for you mother, in more ways than one," she said out loud as she put the frame down. There were places she had to go, people, she had to see.

***

Derrick Wade was not letting go. If Kato thought that she could pull the rug out from under him by firing him, she was sadly mistaken. It made him that much more determined to find out about her past and now, with no job, he had that much more time to devote to it.

His sources at the hospital either didn't know anything or they simply weren't talking. He would just have to march right into the hospital and find things out for himself. Okay, maybe sneak in, but nonetheless, he was going to get the information he wanted.

***

The alterations were complete, and the dress had just been delivered. Kato couldn't wait to try it on to make sure it fit. Many designers had tried to convince her to wear one of their creations to the big event, but she had turned them all down. She had known for a long time what she had wanted to wear. It was an emerald-green dress made of the finest silk, and now with the alterations, it was a perfect fit. Its lines were classic and timeless; it's off the shoulder design showing an expanse of throat and shoulders. It had been her mother's favourite dress. She looked at the star necklace that Toma had given her. It shone brilliantly and was the only adornment that she needed that night.

***

Jackpot! Derrick felt like he had just won the lottery. It had taken him hours of going through files, but he had finally found what he was looking for, and it was mind-boggling. Kato was Cassandra Carrington! The file showed she had gone through extensive surgeries after being a victim of a vicious stabbing. Derrick knew exactly what he was going to do with this information, but first he had to confirm it with police records. He couldn't get this wrong, too much depended on it.

***

The big night had finally arrived! Kato took extra care with her appearance, almost making a ritual of it. She coiled her hair onto the top of her head, then maneuvered the wig over it. She checked her hairline for any stray copper coloured hairs and was careful to tuck all of them under the wig. It was show time!

***

Kato stepped out of the limousine, bracing herself against the lights and the cameras. A reporter approached her and stated, "You've come alone this evening." Kato smiled and said suggestively, "Yes, but I'm not planning on leaving alone." and with that, she gave the reporter a wink and continued up the red carpet.

***

Viktor had been sitting at home in front of his television and had caught Kato's little quip. But it wasn't her witty statement that made him smile, it was the fact that she didn't have an escort by her side. There was hope for him yet. He found himself sitting on the edge of his seat. He had seen her latest movie, Kato deserved to win.

***

Kato was sitting with other members of the cast of "Midnight Mission of Angels" and when the nominees for the best leading female actor were announced, they all gave her encouraging smiles. But Kato didn't notice, she had her head bowed. In two swift movements, she had removed the contacts from her eyes and threw them into her evening bag.

She heard the announcer on the stage, "The envelope please... and the winner is... Kato!" Kato made her way up to the stage, evening bag in hand. The applause died down, and she began her speech, "This is such an honour. I would like to thank the cast and crew of

'Midnight Mission of Angels'. Without their talent and skill, I wouldn't be up here now, making this speech. I would also not be up here today if it weren't for the encouragement my mother had given me throughout the years. I'm sad to say that she is no longer with us, but I know, in spirit she is with me here tonight, so this is for my mother, Carolyn Carrington!"

The audience was stunned into silence as Casandra removed the dark wig, her own copper coloured hair swinging down over her shoulders. Only one person was not surprised by the disclosure, Charlotte Douglas. Cassandra had called her the day before to tell Charlotte of her plan. Now Charlotte stole a glance at her husband sitting beside her; his face had turned an unbecoming shade of red. She looked down at his hands; his knuckles were white as he tightly gripped the arms of his seat. He didn't even notice when Charlotte slipped away, he was mesmerized by the woman on the stage, the one wearing the green dress that he knew so well. It had been a one-of-a-kind and had belonged to Carolyn Carrington. His face paled and turned the same shade of white as his knuckles.

Cassandra took advantage of the silence to continue, "Yes, I'm Cassandra Carrington, daughter of Carolyn Carrington, but I'm also the daughter of Carlyle Douglas, the man who murdered my mother!" The audience let out an audible gasp. Carlyle was flabbergasted and defiant at the same time. She had no proof!

Cassandra pulled an envelope out of her evening bag and continued, "You see, I brought my own envelope here tonight, the envelope that holds the sympathy card that Carlyle Douglas had mailed to me, the morning *of the same* day of the evening of her death. The envelope that I am now going to hand over to the police". On cue, a police officer came over to Cassandra on the stage, and she handed it over to him.

Carlyle had heard enough; he was getting out. He got up to make a break for it and only then did he notice that the entire row of seats he was sitting in had been emptied out. At each end of the row, there were police officers. He collapsed down onto his seat. He was trapped.

Cassandra was still on the stage when the police took Carlyle away. She thanked the audience for indulging her and then left the stage, Oscar in hand.

Chapter 18

Viktor was blown away! Wow! And he thought a lot had happened in his life! Cassandra must have been going through a private hell. To find out that her mother had been murdered, and by one's own father, and that father is Carlyle Douglas. Boy, to tell it all before millions, that was gutsy! Viktor was feeling gutsy himself; it was time to make a move.

***

The press had gone wild. Video cameras were rolling, and camera bulbs flashed as the entourage of police officers ushered Carlyle Douglas out of the building in handcuffs. Two officers were holding him; all the rest were keeping the crowd at bay. Then, as if on cue, police cars pulled up in front just as the officers with Carlyle reached the curb. Before the reporters could find out what was going on, Cassandra had already slipped out and into her waiting limousine.

***

Home at last. It had been a highly emotionally charged night for Cassandra, and it had drained all of the energy out of her. She placed her Oscar on her bedside table before plopping down on her bed still fully dressed.

She had done it! She had won the Oscar, and exposed Carlyle Douglas! She just wished she could have seen his face, but he had been sitting too far away. Cassandra felt victorious, but it was short-lived. She thought of the trial that would follow, would he be convicted and get what he deserved? Would justice prevail?

The doorbell rang. Who the heck? Cassandra dragged herself off of the bed and headed for the door. "Viktor!" she exclaimed. Viktor didn't wait for an invitation but walked through the doorway. Words couldn't express what he felt, so he simply caught Cassandra up in a passionate embrace. Cassandra responded, her body molding to him, her passion rising to match his. He unzipped the green dress, and it fell to the floor. He couldn't bear to let go of her for a single second. Still in an embrace he used his arms to raise her up off of the floor. She wrapped her legs around him, and he carried her down the hallway to her bedroom.

Cassandra awoke slowly, her eyes hadn't focused yet, and it took her awhile to make out the strange object on her bedside table. Her Oscar! So it hadn't been a dream. But as much as she had been thrilled to claim it and take it home, she would trade it any day for the man who, at this very moment, had his arm across her body as he slept. She smiled, she decided it was time for the sleepy-head to rise and shine.

Cassandra was about to turn her body around when something odd about the Oscar caught her eye. She reached over and picked up the object balanced on top of the statue's head. She held it with her fingers and studied it; then her eyes opened wide. Even in the dim light, the emerald set in the platinum band shone brightly.

Viktor stirred behind her. He raised himself up on one arm and kissed her neck, "Marry me?" he asked. Cassandra turned and faced him and managed a low, husky "Yes". Her kiss said the rest.

***

Cassandra was perspiring under the hot studio lights. One person touched up her makeup while another fussed over her hair. She had to admit that without the cover of her contacts and a dark wig, she felt vulnerable and exposed. She started to get impatient; she just wanted to get the interview over and done with. She smiled. At least, the interview was going to happen on her turf and on her terms. She had decided the best way to get her story out was for her to go public, although already she was limited by what she could say regarding the murder trial. Carlyle Douglas' lawyers had quickly instigated a gag order.

***

Derrick Wade was frustrated beyond words! Had he gotten his information sooner, the whole thing would have turned out differently for him. He would have been basking in glory, having uncovered Kato for who she really was, but now the information was useless. He had to admit, though, that the news he had been going to announce wasn't anywhere near as sensational as what Cassandra Carrington herself had revealed.

Derrick watched her now on the television. He studied her closely as she told her story. She was calm and collected and... there was something in her body language... she was hiding something! And he wasn't going to rest until he found out what it was!

***

Damn the woman to hell! Cassandra had been a thorn in his side since the day she was born. Carlyle had tolerated her mother Carolyn only because she had held Cassandra over his head, and it seemed that now, all of that was for not. Apparently his wife had known about Carolyn and Cassandra the whole time. Then when he thought he had managed to remove both Carolyn and Cassandra from his life, they came back to haunt him, Carolyn from the grave, Cassandra in the flesh. And to think how Cassandra must have been laughing at him the whole time, how he had almost begged her to be in his last two movies.

Carlyle paced back and forth within the confines of the four walls he was imprisoned in. He thought of what his life was now reduced to, and it was all her fault! Carlyle slumped down onto the narrow cot and put his head in his hands. He was a defeated man, and he felt there was only one way out. He knew exactly who could help him end this nightmare he was living, but the thought gave him no solace.

***

"Hey! Over here!" Cassandra could hear Karen calling her but couldn't catch sight of her as she glanced around the restaurant. She finally noticed her waving her arms frantically. The girls had decided to get together for lunch to celebrate Jen's and Cassandra's engagements. She headed to the corner table where Karen, Jen, Vera, and Barbara were already sitting. Jen was the first one to greet her, "Congratulations on your engagement Kato, I mean Cassandra, gee, that's going to take some getting used to." Vera has some great news too." Karen interjected. Jen piped in, "Ya, she's pregnant!" Vera was put out, "Hey, just because I'm pregnant doesn't mean I've forgotten how to talk!" "We should be so lucky." Barbara teased.

The banter continued, but Casandra wasn't listening. Vera was expecting. It was great news, and she was happy for her, but Cassandra couldn't help but feel a bit empty. As a result of the stabbing by Fraser, Cassandra might never be able to carry to full term. She and

Viktor had discussed it, and he said he was fine with it if they never had children. He said it was her that he wanted, not a baby machine. She was sure that he had meant it when he said it but, whenever she watched him with his niece, Cassandra had to wonder.

Vera had dropped out of the conversation and noticed Cassandra's silence. Of course, how insensitive of them all. She walked around and put her hands comfortingly on Cassandra's shoulders, "Don't worry, your day will come, I'm sure of it." Cassandra gave Vera a small smile. Vera, in turn, gave Cassandra's shoulders an encouraging squeeze. Cassandra was able to shake the melancholy and was able to enjoy the rest of the evening.

***

Cassandra walked through the cemetery towards her mother's grave. She knelt down beside the headstone and placed a bouquet of white lilies in front of it. A shadow fell over the grave, and Cassandra looked up to the sky. Dark clouds had formed, and the wind had picked up. Afraid that the lilies might blow away, she reached her hand down to cover them but discovered that they had taken root. But they were no longer beautiful and white, but withered and dead. Only the roots were alive, growing, taking over the earth and disturbing it. The roots began to act like gnarled fingers, lifting her mother's casket up out of the ground. Cassandra grabbed one end of it pulling with all of her might. The tug-of-war continued, and her arms grew weak, and then just when she felt she couldn't hold on any longer the casket broke apart, her mother's body falling to the ground. Cassandra rushed to her mother's body, reaching out to touch it, but then recoiled in horror. It wasn't her mother; it was Carlyle Douglas.

Cassandra woke up with a start; her body drenched in sweat. She looked over at the clock; it was nine-fifteen. She inched her body away from Viktor's, being careful not to disturb him. She slipped off of the bed and headed to the bathroom to have a shower.

***

Cassandra came out of the shower feeling like a new woman and was ready to take on the world. She returned to the bedroom but stopped short when she saw Viktor. He was sitting up in bed, looking serious. "What's wrong?" she asked. He motioned her to sit beside him on the bed, "The prosecution called while you were in the shower. There isn't going to be a trial." She was stunned. No trial? But everything was all set to go. What could have possibly have happened for everything to change? She opened her mouth to speak, but before she could Viktor spoke, "There won't be any trial because Carlyle is dead, he committed suicide."

Viktor took Casandra in his arms and held her tight while the news sunk in. He wasn't sure how she was going to react to the news. He personally was glad the man was dead, in fact, he would like to shake the hand of the person who had smuggled in the drugs that allowed Carlyle to end his life. His death was going to save Cassandra a lot of personal anguish, having to testify in court, resurrecting memories of her mother's death.

Cassandra didn't know what she felt. Relieved maybe that it had come to an end, perhaps cheated somehow, that justice hadn't been done, but then again, maybe it had.

***

"Sorry, but do I know you?" Cassandra asked the person on the other end of the phone line. "It's Miss Templeton, Carlyle Douglas' secretary, or I guess former secretary now." Cassandra had to wonder why Carlyle's secretary would be contacting her. She wouldn't tell Cassandra what it was about on the phone but told Cassandra that it would be best if Cassandra could come to the studio. Cassandra found it all very cryptic but agreed to meet with her at the studio all the same.

***

Cassandra met Jane Templeton in Carlyle's office, and Jane asked her to sit down. Jane then walked over to a safe on the wall. It must have been unlocked earlier because all Jane did now was pull on the handle to open the door and take out some papers. She handed them to Cassandra. Cassandra was puzzled. Jane explained, "I know you were told that your money was gone, but that wasn't completely true. You see, Carlyle had let your mother buy stock in the studio. He then offered to hold on to them for safe-keeping. He obviously never intended for her to get them back. But here they are, they're yours now."

It all looked legitimate enough, and being the sole beneficiary of her mother's will; there was no question that they now belonged to her. Jane went on to say that she had known about the shares but didn't know where they were located until she had brought in a locksmith to have the safe opened after Carlyle's death. Jane added, "Also, I had no way of contacting you. Shortly after your mother's death, you seemed to have disappeared off of the face of the earth." Something like that thought Cassandra.

"Oh, there's another reason why I asked you to come here today. I'll have to ask that you follow me." Jane took a set of keys from the pocket of her blazer and motioned for Cassandra to follow her. She led her down a corridor and stopped in front of a door near the end of it. She unlocked and opened the door, then flicked on the light. It was a supply room, and Jane went to the back of the room and started to pull out large mail bags from behind a shelving unit. She had pulled out five in all and explained, "Mr. Douglas had instructed me to destroy these, but I couldn't bring myself to do it." Cassandra looked at the bags in puzzlement.

Jane opened one of the bags and pulled out a handful of envelopes, "It's fan mail you received in the care of the studio, mostly from when your mother had passed away. It's all here in these bags." Cassandra put her hands to her face, overcome with emotion. Those years since her mother passed away, she thought that no one had cared. Now she knew otherwise. Those bags of mail meant more to her than any shares in Carlyle Douglas' company ever would.

***

Cassandra spent the better part of the day reading through the letters, and she hadn't even made a dent in them. She was overwhelmed by many of them. Some brought tears to her eyes; others made her smile. They reminded her of the most important part of being an actor, the fans. She came to a decision. She wanted to star in another movie. But first, she had other plans to bring to fruition, wedding plans. She looked at the clock; Viktor would be there any time now, and she wasn't anywhere near ready. She hastily gathered up the letters. They had been sitting unopened for years; they could wait a few more weeks to be read.

***

Well, this was a turn of events that she hadn't anticipated. Charlotte Douglas had managed to get her husband out of the way, and with her son out of the picture too, everything went to her. Everything that is except for half of the production company. That was one thing that her dearly departed husband had managed to keep from her. How could he have sold out to Carolyn Carrington? Now Charlotte found herself in business with Carolyn's daughter. As far as Charlotte was concerned, Cassandra had served her purpose. But having her as a business partner was another story. Charlotte found the whole situation very distasteful.

***

It was going to be a Fourth of July to remember. The fireworks were on a barge, all set to go off at the signal. Guests were boarding the private yacht as the sun set. "Isn't this exciting?" squealed Jen. Karen replied, "I have to admit, I have butterflies in my stomach!" The yacht started to leave the port, and everyone moved to the railing to wave at the crowd that had gathered on shore. They stayed there for quite a while, waving and cheering, but once the people on the dock were tiny dots in the distance, the guests on the yacht got into position. The engine stopped, and the minister stood, bible in hand. Then on cue, the wedding march began.

Viktor's breath was taken away as he watched Cassandra walk towards him. Her oyster coloured dress hugged her curves down to her knees, then flared out, sweeping the carpet that had been laid down for the occasion. The strapless dress showed off her creamy shoulders and at her throat was the string of pearls that had belonged to her mother. She wore no veil, but strings of tiny freshwater pearls were woven into her hair. Viktor thought he was looking at a vision, a mermaid that had risen from the sea. He had indeed found a rare treasure.

Cassandra stopped at Viktor's side. She thought her heart would burst from happiness. Looking at Viktor, she couldn't think of anything she wanted more in the world than to have this man by her side for the rest of her life. They joined hands and looked to the minister. The ceremony began. It wasn't a long ceremony, but what it lacked in length, it made up for in heart. They had written their own vows, and their voices shook from emotion as they exchanged them. They became husband and wife and as they kissed the fireworks lit up the night sky.

***

The celebration continued into the night, and it was early morning before the yacht headed back to shore to drop off the wedding guests. Cassandra and Viktor again thanked the guests for coming as each one of them disembarked. With all of the guests on shore, the yacht headed back out in the open water, taking Cassandra and Viktor with it.

***

It was a glorious two weeks, but it was time to get back to the reality of everyday life. As they headed to their destination, both began having thoughts that invaded their idyllic world.

Cassandra couldn't get out of her mind the fact that she had a meeting the next day with her new business partner Charlotte Douglas. She didn't even want to hazard a guess as to what the other woman had to propose.

Viktor looked at the shore that they were fast approaching. Once back on land, the honeymoon was definitely going to be over, or at least, put on hiatus for a few weeks. He had to go out of town on business and just hoped that he could wrap things up in a three-week time frame. He couldn't bear the thought of being away from Cassandra for even that long.

They had been standing side by side at the railing, but now Viktor moved behind her and held her tightly against him. Cassandra leaned back, letting her head rest against his broad chest. Neither wanted ever to let go.

Chapter 19

Charlotte Douglas wanted out, and she told Cassandra as much. Cassandra weighed her options. She could hang on to her shares of the production company and take her chances with several other potential shareholders, or one other shareholder if someone came and bought all of Charlotte's shares. Another option for Cassandra was to sell her shares, the same as Charlotte intended to do. She could also make the choice to buy Charlotte out. Cassandra was considering the last option.

***

It didn't take Cassandra long to decide to buy out Charlotte, and now the entire production company, studio and all belonged to her. She should have been elated, but she found the whole situation daunting. She was an actor; she knew nothing of running a company.

***

Her dry spell had gone on way too long, and in order to keep her supply of drugs coming, Veronica Sutton needed money. She had hawked her computer, and now she was reduced to checking the want ads in the newspaper. She had just finished looking through the classified section of the paper when she saw the article in the business section. Cassandra Cross was now sole owner of what was now called "Crossroads Cinema." That was the end of any chances Veronica may have had to star in any movies with that company. She had definitely burned her bridges there.

The phone rang, and Veronica jumped and was tempted to answer it after the first ring, but held back and let it ring three more times, "Hello, Veronica Sutton here." It was a job offer, one that she had received a few times before, but had always turned down in disdain. This time, when it was offered she accepted, she needed money for more drugs.

Veronica hung up and immediately thought of calling back and saying that she had changed her mind about doing the porn movie, but then her hands started to shake, she needed a fix, and she needed one now.

***

A screenplay had come across Cassandra's desk that had caught her eye. It was a period piece, and she could see herself playing the lead character of Emily, an unmarried woman by choice, in a time when such a life-choice for a single woman was unheard of. It was totally different from her last two movie roles, so it would be a challenge. But how could she swing it? Since she had taken charge of the company all of her time had been dedicated to running it.

There was a knock on the door. Cassandra said loudly, "Come in." Jane Templeton opened the door and poked her head in, "Sorry to bother you, I just wanted to know if you wanted me to pick up some lunch for you." Cassandra had told her "no thanks", but as Jane was about to close the door, Cassandra added, "but there is something you *can* do for me."

It was the opportunity Jane had dreamed about ever since she had started with the company over twenty years ago. Jane was now in charge, and Cassandra had given her a new title and a hefty raise. She was also going to have her own office, Carlyle Douglas' old office, and had permission to redecorate it as she saw fit. Jane walked around the office with a large cardboard box, removing any remaining traces of Carlyle Douglas.

***

With her time freed up, Cassandra was able to start production on the movie. Everything was taking so much time. After an extensive search, the cast had finally been picked, but the costumes were going to take some time to create as they were going to be quite elaborate. It looked like Cassandra was going to have to bide her time, so she decided to take advantage of the lull in her schedule to do some shopping and pick up a Christmas gift for her husband. Her husband. This was going to be their first Christmas together as husband and wife. She wanted it to be special, and she knew the gift she was going to get him was something that he wanted more than anything. However, the gift wasn't something she could pick up from a department store.

***

Viktor was at a loss. What did you get a woman who has everything? He thought of one thing she had lost and was now missing from her life. Viktor decided work could wait, for now; he had a Christmas gift to pick out.

***

For the most part, Cassandra and Viktor resided in the house that Cassandra had inherited from Toma. Their decision had stemmed from convenience more than anything else, and although they spent most of their time there, on occasion, they would stay at Viktor's home. They had decided to stay at his place over the Christmas holidays. Cassandra was glad. Toma's house held too many memories of him. At Viktor's it would be like a fresh start with new Christmas, memories to be made.

Cassandra and Viktor had gone all out, hanging garland, putting up lights and putting up an enormous tree. They had just finished decorating it, and the glass ornaments sparkled in the light from both the twinkling mini-lights on the tree and from the flames that crackled in the fireplace. There was just one last thing to be done. Viktor walked over to the door frame and reaching up, hung the mistletoe. Cassandra was by his side, and as he lowered his arm, he placed it around her, and then they kissed. Their first kiss was a playful little peck, and then, as their kisses continued, they became more passionate. They no longer noticed the colourful trimmings or the twinkling lights. Even the flickering flames that warmed their skin went unnoticed. The heat from the fire couldn't compete with the heat from Cassandra's and Viktor's inner fires as they touched.

***

Cassandra awoke Christmas morning expecting to find Viktor beside her, but his side of the bed was empty, empty and cold. What kind of Christmas was this? She got out of bed and went to the kitchen. That was empty too. She set off for the living room.

Viktor could hear Cassandra coming down the hallway; he had to act fast. He had just got in five minutes earlier and hadn't had a chance to get everything in place. He hurriedly pushed the package he had brought home with him behind a large armchair and dove for the stereo, turning the Christmas music up loud, just as Cassandra got to the doorway.

Cassandra leaned against the door frame and had to smile. He was just like a little kid, wide awake and eager to open up his Christmas present. He came over to where she stood, taking advantage of the mistletoe over their heads. But he made the kiss brief this morning because, even with the loud music playing, he could hear some scratching sounds. He took Cassandra's hand and led her to the Christmas tree, instructing her to sit on the floor and close her eyes.

Cassandra wondered what was going on, but did as Viktor had asked. When he told her to open her eyes, she found a large box decorated with Christmas wrapping paper. The lid was also decorated but was just sitting loosely on the top of the box. She lifted it slowly and leaned in to see its contents. This gift was not like any other that she had ever received. Never before had her gifts looked back at her with big brown eyes. It was a puppy! A Great Dane that, at the sight of her, put its paws on the side of the box and tried to scamper out.

Cassandra squealed with delight as she picked the puppy up and held it in her arms. She was so absorbed with the little furry bundle that she had almost forgotten about giving Viktor his gift. She placed the puppy back into the open box for the time being, reached under the Christmas tree and picked up a flat, brightly decorated package. She hoped that he would be as enthusiastic about it as she was.

As Viktor accepted the gift, he wondered what could be inside. He ripped the wrapping paper off to reveal an envelope. The envelope was sealed, and he had to tear it to get to the contents. It was the application forms needed to be completed in order to adopt. They had discussed the possibility at great length, but Cassandra had been holding back, hoping that, eventually, she would become pregnant. It hadn't happened, and now this was her way of saying she was willing to go ahead with adoption proceedings. He couldn't have asked for a better gift.

***

The holiday season came and went, and it was life as usual. The shooting for Cassandra's film had started, and Viktor was back and forth on various business trips. They had been told that it could be months, even years before the adoption agency could place a baby with them, and having heard that news they both had reacted by concentrating on their respective careers. Their work days were long, and it seemed that the only time that they had to spend together was when they would take the puppy for a walk along the beach.

The puppy was all black in colour and had been growing by leaps and bounds. They had called him MacKenzie and at first, they had called him Mac for short, but now, because of the size he had grown to and was still growing, they had nicknamed him Big Mac. He was good therapy for them; he filled the gap left by the absence of a child.

***

It was late October and the last day of shooting when Cassandra received the call. She had left instructions with the office that she was to be interrupted no matter what when the call came in. Although she had been on the set at the time, she wasn't in the scene, and she was able to slip away unobserved. She was elated as she hung up and couldn't wait to tell Viktor the news!

***

***

She was sixteen years old and three months pregnant. She wanted to give the child up to a good home, all she asked was that her medical costs were covered. Cassandra and Viktor had no problem complying with that condition. By April, they were going to be parents!

***

Cassandra's movie "A Desire to Fight For" was in post-production and Viktor had cleared his schedule. This Christmas they were going to give each other a gift of a trip to New Zealand. They figured that if they didn't get away for this time together, they never would, what with a child coming into their lives in April. They were all packed and ready to go and were just waiting for Karen to get there as she had volunteered to look after MacKenzie for them.

Karen sped up the driveway in her Honda Civic. She got out, running up to the house and apologized profusely, urging them, "Hurry! Go! You don't want to miss your flight!" Cassandra and Viktor didn't argue, they handed her the house keys and were on their way.

***

It was a glorious summer day in Wellington as their plane touched down. Cassandra and Viktor stayed a few days there before they traveled on to other regions to take in more sights. They had a glorious time, hiking, mountain climbing and even fishing.

Viktor had really been looking forward to the fishing and was bragging that he was going to catch himself a big one, but as it turned out, Cassandra had been the one to catch a large swordfish, and she made sure that they had the photographs to prove it. She wasn't going to let him live that one down for a long time to come.

***

Their vacation came to an end and all too soon they were back home. They checked their answering machine, and there were messages for both of them. One of Viktor's stated that he was needed in Reno to close a deal, another was that he was needed at the office ASAP because of some complications that had arisen. Cassandra had only one message, post-production on "A Desire to Fight For" had finally been completed.

***

Everyone who had previewed the film agreed, "A Desire to Fight For" should be submitted to the Cannes Film Festival. Cassandra was elated; she could hardly wait until May!

***

As much as Cassandra was looking forward to May, she was even more excited about April. She brushed a strand of hair from her face, then continued to affix the colourful border to the wall. Viktor came into the room just as she had put the last piece up, "Looking good!" She replied, "Not too shabby a job if I do say so myself." "Who said I was talking about the room?" Viktor asked suggestively. They stood in the middle of the room, both looking forward to April.

***

Cassandra was holding her new son in her arms. She was singing a lullaby as she rocked him to sleep in her arms. She was expecting Viktor to return home at any time, and when the door opened, she called out to him, "We're in the nursery Viktor." She could hear footsteps getting closer, but it wasn't Viktor who appeared in the doorway. A young woman stood there, staring at her and the baby. Without a word the woman walked towards Cassandra, snatching the baby from her arms. Cassandra ran after the woman, but as she tried to catch her, the young woman turned into a vulture. It flew in the air; the baby clutched in its talons. Cassandra could hear the baby's screams and she fell to her knees, praying that the child would be returned to her. With the baby still in its grasp, the vulture began to circle overhead, waiting, watching, looking for any sign of weakness from Cassandra.

Cassandra awoke. She was so deeply affected by the disturbing images in her dream that she felt physically ill. She couldn't stop shaking. Being careful not to wake Viktor, she got out of bed and walked down the hallway and into the nursery. She picked up a teddy bear that was in the crib and sat down in the rocking chair. Holding the stuffed toy to her, she rocked back and forth until she finally rocked herself to sleep.

***

Cassandra and Viktor were both home when the call came in. The young mother-to-be had changed her mind. The adoption agency apologized profusely, but it didn't alleviate their grief. They were devastated.

Cassandra could understand the young woman changing her mind; she probably would have done the same in that situation. But then she thought, no, she wouldn't have done the same as the young woman, she would never have considered putting her child up for adoption in the first place. As much as she respected the young woman's decision, Cassandra could not be comforted, even Viktor's strong arms around her could not ease the pain in her heart.

***

Cassandra and Viktor felt like they were in mourning. Even with the door shut tight, they found it difficult to walk past the nursery. The adoption agency had tried to be encouraging, saying that it shouldn't take long for another opportunity to come along, but they were skeptical. What if the same thing happened to them all over again? They wouldn't be able to handle the heartache, not again. But then, what choice did they have?

***

Cassandra and Viktor were greeted by hoards of people and the press as they stepped out of the airport in France. The Cannes Film Festival was taking place, and the excitement was all around them. It was infectious, and Cassandra felt herself getting caught up in the moment, she turned impulsively to Viktor and planted a big kiss on his lips. Cameras clicked and captured the moment, but Cassandra didn't care, she was in love, and she didn't care who knew it.

***

At first, Cassandra hadn't minded, but as the festival wore on, the press made her feel claustrophobic. No matter where she and Viktor went, there they were. Even as they strolled along the Croisette, the press was there. She couldn't wait until it was all over.

***

The wait had been well worth it, "A Desire to Fight For" with its superior acting, and elaborate costumes and sets, had been dubbed a masterpiece had been awarded the prestigious *Pale D'or*! Cassandra could think of no higher honour. She settled in beside Vikor on the plane and then they were on their way home.

Cassandra had dozed off, and Viktor studied her face as she slept. She looked so unpretentious; it was hard to believe that she was such a famous woman. She never ceased to amaze him. He had to wonder what she would accomplish next.

***

Cassandra was shocked by the news. It had never entered her mind that she might be presented with such an honour. She was going to get her very own bronze star on the Hollywood Walk of Fame that was located along Hollywood Boulevard and Vine Street. The ceremony was gong to take place the following month, on the first of July, her birthday. She couldn't have asked for a better birthday present.

Viktor couldn't have been happier for Cassandra, but he had to wonder about one thing, what name was she going to want to immortalize? After revealing to the world who she really was at the Academy Awards. she had changed her first name from Kato back to Cassandra, and had taken his last name Cross when they were married, but would she want to use her maiden name of Carrington? She had, after all, started in acting and had won an Oscar under that name. He didn't want her to feel obligated to use the name Cross, especially as she might want to use Carrington in her mother's honour. Viktor had to talk to her about it.

***

Cassandra held Viktor to her. How could he ever have thought that she wouldn't want to use his name? Carrington was in the past, Cross was who she was now, and Cross would be the name that she would have proudly displayed on her star. Viktor would never admit it to Cassandra, but he was secretly pleased about her decision. He became deep in thought. He was going to have to come up with something special to mark this momentous event.

***

Derrick Wade knew it was just a matter of time before he found out what Cassandra Carrington, now Cassandra Cross, had been trying to keep buried in her past.

While checking into her violent stabbing, Derrick had come across some other interesting information from police records. Two separate cases, but the pieces of the puzzle fit. It was now a well-known fact that Carlyle Douglas and Cassandra Carrington were father and daughter, so she would have known Carlyle's son Fraser. Had Cassandra had an affair with her half-brother? When Cassandra was attacked, her Doberman pup had been left to hang on the hook on the bathroom door. Fraser had gone overseas shortly after the stabbing incident. Fraser returns to America and attends a party that Cassandra also attends. Next thing you know, Fraser turns up dead, attacked by that same Doberman.

Derrick didn't quite believe the note Toma Kato had written about leaving the gate open that fateful night, it seemed a bit too convenient for him. Even without the proof, Derrick's gut told him that the truth was yet to be uncovered, and he was going to be the one to uncover it. Once he knew the truth, he knew exactly what he was going to do with the information.

Derrick was still out of work, and in order to survive, he had resorted to blackmail in more than one instance. Even now, there were a few people that he was extorting money from, but this, this was big. He had found the mother lode! He would be able to collect money for years from Cassandra Cross, and then, once he bled her dry, he could sell the story. With such a sensational story, he was bound to get some cushy job offers out of it too. Derrick decided it was time to make his phone call.

Chapter 20

The Walk of Fame ceremony was only a week away, and Viktor had never seen Cassandra so jittery. Of course, who could blame her, it was a huge honour to be awarded a star. He just hoped that she could make it through the week without having a nervous breakdown.

***

To think that a few days ago she had been on top of the world, now for Cassandra it felt like her world was falling apart. It was all because of a phone call from Derrick Wade. He had made it quite clear to her that it was blackmail money he wanted, and lots of it. She had been too stunned to think even of a response at the time never mind a decision. Derrick had told her that she had three days to think about it. He would contact her again then, and she had better have come to a decision, the *right* decision.

One day had already passed, and Cassandra still hadn't decided what to do. All she knew was that she couldn't go to jail, she had too many reasons for wanting, no, *needing* her freedom.

***

She traveled to a seedy area of the city. Even though she knew she wouldn't run into anyone she knew in this area of town, she still found herself keeping an eye out for familiar faces as she entered the shabby little shop.

The man behind the counter knew what she had come for the second she walked through the door wearing the plain coat, dark glasses, and hat, the wide brim pulled down low to cover as much of her face as possible. She was here for a gun. She picked out a small one, something discrete that would fit into a handbag.

As the clerk watched her walk out the door, he had to wonder who the bullet was meant for. His guess was a cheating husband. But hey, what did he care? He had gotten his money and a lot of it at that. That bullet was a problem that belonged to someone else.

***

It was a miserable night, the wind was blowing, and the rain was coming down hard. She couldn't help but think that it was freakishly cold for June. She pulled the collar of her coat closer around her throat; she was probably going to get a miserable cold before the night was through. She was tempted to go into the dive of a bar that was next door to warm up, but she didn't want to take the chance of anyone seeing or being able to identify her. So instead, she stood in the back alley, waiting.

Where was he? She had told him she would give him the money, here, tonight, but he still hadn't shown. She looked at her watch. It wasn't her imagination; he was late, by half-an-hour. Even though she was wearing gloves, her hands were still cold. She put them in her pockets, not only for warmth but to conceal the gun she held in her right hand.

***

Vikor was normally a deep sleeper but tonight, with the howling wind and the rain pelting against the bedroom window, he had a fitful sleep. It was no use; he might as well give up on getting back to sleep. He turned over to see if Cassandra had been awakened by the storm, only to find her side of the bed empty. He got up and walked past the bathroom, study, living room and kitchen, but she wasn't anywhere to be found.

He was debating where to check next when the kitchen door leading outside opened wide. Cassandra came through the doorway, her hair plastered to her head, her clothes dripping wet. He was about to ask her where she had been when MacKenzie bounded in after her. He suddenly felt guilty, how could he have forgotten about the poor dog, outside in this weather? They did have a dog house for him, but he tended not to use it. He looked just as cold and wet as Cassandra.

Viktor ordered, "Into the shower with you, we don't want you getting sick for your big day." Cassandra couldn't argue with that; she didn't want to risk getting sick.

***

Viktor had to get up early to go to the office, but Cassandra lingered in bed long after he had gone. Finally, her stomach began to growl, and she had no choice but to head to the kitchen for something to eat.

What did she want for breakfast? Nothing seemed to appeal to her. She finally decided on just a bowl of cereal. The house seemed quiet without Viktor there, so she turned on the small television in the kitchen before she sat down to eat. "... *the body was discovered when a patron of a nearby bar had stumbled into the alley. The man has been identified as twenty-eight-year-old Derrick Wade, former reporter of "The Limelight". Time of death was estimated to be at 2:00 am...*"

Cassandra dropped her spoon into her cereal bowl, splattering milk everywhere.

***

It was past noon by the time Charlotte Douglas woke up. As she lay in bed, she started to shiver. She could feel a cold coming on, but she didn't care, it had been worth it. She had allowed Derrick Wade to extort money from her, but not anymore. She had no idea how he had gotten the incriminating evidence that proved she had provided the lethal pills that had ended her husband's life, but he had. The police had concluded that it had been a case of contraband somehow getting into the prison, which wasn't uncommon and pretty much impossible to trace. Charlotte had taken it upon herself to ensure their theory remained intact.

Charlotte had felt like a prisoner for years, living under the overbearing presence of Carlyle Douglas, and now that she had her freedom there was no way that anyone was going to take it away from her. It wasn't long after she had married the man that she had regretted having signed that damn prenuptial agreement. She let out a forceful sneeze that racked her whole body. She grabbed a facial tissue from her bedside table and pulled the covers up around her neck. As soon as she was feeling better she was going to book an appointment at a spa, maybe somewhere in the south of France.

***

Cassandra jumped when the phone rang. She was expecting an important call and snatched the receiver up on the first ring. It was a brief call, but it didn't take long to find out what she wanted to know. After she had hung up she made her own phone call; she had a cancellation to make.

Cassandra couldn't have asked for better timing, what with the Walk of Fame ceremony tomorrow, and her birthday. She could hardly wait for her big day!

***

Viktor was so proud of Cassandra as she stood there before the cameras. Not only was she beautiful and poised, but she was also humble and sincere in accepting the honour being bestowed on her. As happy as he was for her and her moment in the spotlight, he couldn't wait to get her home and have him all to himself.

***

It had been an exceptional day and Cassandra was practically vibrating she was so excited. And the thing was, the best was yet to come. Once she and Viktor arrived home, she dragged him into the study. It took him by surprise, but he went along willingly enough.

In the study, Cassandra went over to the desk and opened the top drawer. She pulled out some papers and held them up in front of her. He could see that they were copies of the paperwork that they had filled out to set adoption proceedings in motion. He stood there, motionless, in a state of shock as she took the papers and tore them in half. Before he could react, she threw her arms up in the air, sending the papers flying everywhere and announced, "I'm pregnant!"

Viktor couldn't describe what he felt as he gathered Cassandra up in his arms; it was like he was on a natural high, one he never wanted to come down from.

Vikor wasn't aware of how long they had stood there, locked in an embrace, but he finally came back to the here and now. In all of the excitement, he had forgotten all about the surprise he had planned for Cassandra.

The last thing Viktor wanted to do was leave Cassandra's arms, but he had to. He gave her a quick kiss on her forehead and told her to stay put, that he would be right back. He rushed to their bedroom and to the closet where he reached up and grabbed a present from the top shelf. It was wrapped in dark blue paper and was tied up with a silver coloured ribbon. He hurried back to the study.

Once Viktor had left, Cassandra touched her stomach, she could hardly believe that she was expecting. The doctor had said that he wanted to monitor the pregnancy closely due to her past medical history, but otherwise, he was optimistic. A baby! She thought of her own childhood, of her mother and how her mother had dedicated her life to her. She had to wonder if her mother would have become an actor herself if she hadn't become pregnant. Was that why her mother had been so driven when it came to furthering Cassandra's career?

But if that was the case, could her mother not have pursued acting and been a mother to her at the same time? Many female actors had managed to juggle an acting career with motherhood.

Cassandra would never know what her mother's desires were, but as she caressed her stomach, she knew that she would do everything in her power to help her child achieve his or her dreams.

Viktor returned. He took Cassandra's hand and led her out onto the terrace. It was a perfect night. The moon was full, and the stars shone brightly. He handed the gift to her, "This is to commemorate your special day."

Cassandra untied the ribbon and removed the wrapping paper to reveal what, at first, glance, appeared to be a leather-bound photo album. It had a gold embossed seal and the word "Proclamation" on its cover. She opened it and started to read what was written inside,

To Cassandra Cross

In Celebration of

Receiving your very own star on the "Walk of Fame."

At the Request of

your biggest fan, your husband

You are my Shining Star...

Viktor had registered a star in her name; she had her very own star! Cassandra couldn't speak, and as she finished reading the verse, her eyes brimmed with tears. She looked up into the sky where the twinkling stars seemed to be shining just for her. As she stood there with Viktor by her side, the verse he had chosen for the proclamation went through her mind,

... Star light, star bright

first star I see tonight

I wish I may

I wish I might

become that star

I see tonight.

***

* The End *

Sheila Tracy

ACKNOWLEDGEMENT

To Zoe Duff of Filidh Publishing for believing in me and taking a chance on this first-time author. Kudos to you for having created a publishing company that looks beyond the ordinary and seeks out the unique.

Sheila Tracy

ABOUT THE AUTHOR

Initially, Sheila Tracy utilized her writing skills in the advertising world as a copywriter, but it wasn't until after that time that she was able to focus her creative energies on creating "Star Bright". She hadn't consciously decided to write a book, but rather a storyline kept going through her head and she felt compelled to put it to paper. Being a "Thursday's Child" Sheila always feels that she still has "far to go" and considers "Star Bright" not an end, but the beginning of a new journey.

CPSIA information can be obtained at www.ICGtesting.com
Printed in the USA
LVOW11s2149080616

491674LV00034B/37/P